Praise for
Norma Klein's previous novel,
THAT'S MY BABY

"Philip Roth meets Woody Allen in this wry, breezy Manhattan coming-of-age tale."
The Washington Post

"Written with spunk and insight, THAT'S MY BABY is an affectionate, forgiving portrait of a very young contemporary artist as a very young contemporary man."
Los Angeles Times

"A warm and funny coming-of-age story set against a strong contemporary background . . . When it comes to young adult books, Klein has shown herself to be a writer of great wit and charm."
Publishers Weekly

"Klein's latest bittersweet portrayal of contemporary adolescence will delight readers. . . . Klein tells this story realistically and sympathetically."
Library Journal

JUST FRIENDS

Norma Klein

FAWCETT JUNIPER • NEW YORK

RLI: $\dfrac{\text{VL 6 \& up}}{\text{IL 8 \& up}}$

A Fawcett Juniper Book
Published by Ballantine Books
Copyright © 1990 by the Estate of Norma Klein

All rights reserved under International and Pan-American Copyright Conventions. Published in the United States by Ballantine Books, a division of Random House, Inc., New York, and simultaneously in Canada by Random House of Canada Limited, Toronto.

Library of Congress Catalog Card Number: 89-11148

ISBN 0-449-70352-5

This edition published by arrangement with Alfred A. Knopf, Inc.

Manufactured in the United States of America

First Ballantine Books Edition: March 1991
Fourth Printing: November 1991

To Frances Foster

THE FEARSOME
FOURSOME

It was a late-summer afternoon. The four of us—the "fearsome foursome," as my father called me and my three best girlfriends, Lois, Andria, and Ketti—sat in the living room of my parents' rent-controlled Upper West Side apartment, talking, as we usually did when we were together, about boys. Was it time to start thinking of them, or referring to them, as men? Next year we would be in college, and our college counselor, Ms. Evarts, had come down hard on Lois when she referred to Wells, a college she was thinking of applying to, as "an all-girls college." Actually, it was hard enough thinking of ourselves as women, and nearly impossible to think of the twenty-five boys who would graduate with us in the spring as men.

"I think of Hal as a man," Andria said. If it hadn't been for her edge of wryness and intelligence, Andria would have sounded smug. She was the only one of us who seemed to know exactly where she was going, both in terms of "life" and in terms of her professional goals. She and Hal had been a couple since seventh grade. As far as we knew, they didn't ever have the volatile fights and makings-up that were so

1

frequent with the few other courting couples in our class. At parties they danced together or, sometimes, didn't even dance, just sat and talked, looking more like chaperones, distanced from us by their experience and sophistication. Andria had thick dark hair to her shoulders, heavy black eyebrows, a full but not matronly figure. Next to her Hal, in fact, did look "boyish," slender, quizzical, as though he were relying on her to keep their ship on course.

"Do you think it's because of sex?" Lois asked. "That you think of him that way?" She always asked direct questions like that in an ingenuous, gentle manner. She had gone through school having crushes on some of our teachers or, more rarely, on new boys who would seem, for the moment, mysterious or different. Of the four of us, she and I were "best friends," though these allegiances had shifted over the years. I was quiet and an observer, but Lois was almost pathologically shy. With her I felt bold, jokey. She admired me, and I never went far enough beyond her in terms of experience to create a gap between us. Lois was pale and wispy haired, with round red-rimmed glasses. She refused to try contact lenses because she said the idea of putting something on her eyeball terrified her. A fashion magazine editor would have leaped at the chance to "make her over." I would have been horrified if she'd ever changed.

Andria was sitting cross-legged, knitting. "Sex is just part of a whole," she said in that dignified older-sister way we all admired and resented.

"A hole?" Ketti giggled. "Which one?" If Ketti hadn't been a longtime part of our group—we four and Stuart were the only seniors who had started Whitman together in nursery school—we would have been nervous about her good looks and saucy, daredevil manner. She had a boyfriend a year, at least, "flavor of the month," she jokingly called them. What made me anxious was that Stuart was one of the few presentable boys she hadn't tackled yet, or simply lured by a few well-placed glances.

One tendency I have is to say what's on my mind. This has given me the reputation for being straightforward, which I'm not, totally. I know there are things I can say and no one,

2

except occasionally Lois, will know what I'm getting at. "Who're you aiming for this year?" I asked Ketti. "Stuart?"

She took it as nonchalantly as I'd tried to say it. "Should I? Is he my type?"

Andria looked at her mock-severely. "Who isn't?"

Ketti laughed. "No, it's the opposite, Andria. *None* of them are. That's why I go from guy to guy, hoping for that magical whatever that you and Hal have—I've never had it with anyone! I've had some great sex, fun, good conversations, but never . . ."

Andria and Ketti had a certain status among us because they were not virgins, though Lois and I never felt overly chagrined about our lack of experience. Whitman wasn't that kind of school. To go there you had to be fairly bright, which didn't mean there was no peer pressure, but it was more the kind that revolved around getting a perfect score on your SAT's, or getting your poetry published in the literary magazine, than what you had or hadn't done sexually. Lois and I had noticed that once Andria and Hal started making love consistently, Andria stopped talking about it, at least in a girl-to-girl confiding way. It became something private between her and Hal, the way it was between our parents, if they were still together, like mine, and if we could imagine them doing it at all, which for me was definitely a problem.

"I can see you and Stuart together," Andria said. "Definitely."

"In what way?" Ketti asked. The same question was on my mind, but I wouldn't have voiced it.

Andria squinted. "Well, *you're* zany and fun loving, kind of kooky, but at bottom rock solid, and Stuart seems put together, but with underpinnings of confusion, like he really doesn't know where he's going."

That was, I thought, hideously accurate. Ketti looked pleased. "*Am* I rock solid? Really? I don't know whether to be insulted or pleased."

"You play along with your looks," Andria went on, "because it's attention getting, even though you're smarter than any of us. Look at your math SAT's, or the way you can put puzzles together in one second when we'd be up all night."

3

"I'm afraid boys, men, or what have you will be scared if they know I'm smart," Ketti admitted.

"That's absurd," Andria said. "If you marry someone who thinks he's getting a dizzy blonde, he may freak out when he discovers the truth."

"Marry!" Ketti squealed. "Please. Bite your tongue." Ketti's parents had gone through a bitter divorce four years ago. I always thought her playing the field had as much to do with that as anything, wanting to wreak revenge on guys in retaliation for how her father had treated her mother.

Lois had just been observing this exchange, playing with Andria's ball of wool. "I'm never marrying," she said quietly.

"Why not?" Andria asked.

"I don't know. . . . Guys scare me." Lois cast a quick, shy look at me. We had fooled around together a few years ago, genuinely wondering if we might be gay, liking and trusting each other enough to believe our friendship could survive. There had been good moments, but I had come away with the feeling that what I wanted was something different: a female soul in a male body was as close as I could have come to defining it.

Ketti lay down on the floor. "God, I don't see that. Guys are so—well, pathetic is the wrong word, but it's so easy to manipulate them, especially if they like you. I wish I'd meet someone who'd stand up to me, who wouldn't let me get away with shit all the time."

"Stuart wouldn't," I said. I was always fearful that if I didn't say anything about him, people would notice more than if I did.

"You think? I have a feeling I could make him my helpless slave with a minimum amount of effort." She smiled, as though semitantalized by the prospect.

"Hal isn't Andria's helpless slave," Lois protested.

"He is so!" Ketti said. "Look at the way he looks at her! Aren't I right, Andria?"

Andria looked reflective. She brushed back some stray strands of hair. "I don't think of it in terms of power trips

4

the way you do. We'd both be devastated if the other one . . . if anything happened, and we both know it.''

Ketti smiled at her. "God, you're so commonsensical, it's almost sickening. I want passion, all that rotten, mushy, virulent stuff you read about.''

"Buy a few paperbacks," Andria said, raising an eyebrow. "Or seduce Stuart. Maybe he'll put up more of a struggle than you think." Then, seemingly innocently, she looked at me. "What about you, Iz?''

"What *about* me?''

"Isn't it time? Lois says she's scared, Ketti can't find whatever she thinks she's looking for, but you're kind of a mystery. You seem available, but you never quite—''

"I'm an observer," I said defensively. "It's from being a writer.''

"Bullshit. . . . Anyway, I thought you were going to do premed.''

I'd worked over the summer at a lab at Memorial Hospital, and it was true, molecular biology fascinated me. I'd even written a poem, "Ode to a Pasteur Pipette," but I still thought of myself as a poet. My father, who was an ophthalmologist, said poetry was a fine hobby, but I'd need another way to earn a living, and I thought he was probably right.

"I may, I may not, but do I need to plight my troth right this second? I intend to be a late bloomer.''

Ketti grinned. "Oh come on, Iz. Give it a chance. Bloom now! What have you got to lose?''

"What do I do? Blindfold myself and charge at whoever crosses my path? There's no one who interests me.''

Andria said, "How about Gregory Arrington? He seems like your type. He just needs a little push, a little eyelash batting, the kind of thing Ket could do in her sleep.''

Gregory Arrington was the editor of Whitman's literary magazine. He was a poet, like me, but his poems were weird and surreal—about people melting into rocks, or refrigerators coming to life. He was six feet four with a big Adam's apple and semibad skin. In class he had the answer before anyone, and he loved literary theory, which I loathed.

"Thanks a lot, kid," I said sharply. "*I'm* a female Gregory Arrington? That's a big boost to my ego."

Andria shook her head. "You are *so* hypersensitive. Of course you're not. It's just that you share common interests, you're both kind of tall—"

"I don't have pitted horrendous skin," I fired back, though that was the least of what I minded about Gregory.

"One, his skin has gotten a lot better," Andria countered. "He's gone to some doctor about it. And two, so what? Hal is bowlegged, I have no tits, Ketti's hair has no body . . . I mean, who's into physical perfection here?"

I couldn't help laughing. "Ketti's hair has no body! That's really a major problem, and it sure has caused her no end of trouble with the male sex. Face it, Ketti could be bald, and no one would notice. . . . And don't beg for compliments, Andria. You have breasts to suit your figure. You're Grecian. Your body's just like those statues we saw at the Met."

"*You* said it was his skin," Ketti reminded me.

"No, forget that. He's just— He's like my nightmare image of myself. The teachers adore him, he'll get into Harvard on early admission, he took piano lessons for thirteen years. If he were a scientist, he'd probably win a Westinghouse scholarship. You know what I mean." I was getting more and more heated.

"So what *do* you want?" Ketti said, instead of denying Gregory and I had anything at all in common, as I'd hoped she might.

I stared at her. Stuart, I thought. That's all I want, and all I've ever wanted. "Maybe I'm bisexual," I said, just to get them off the scent. Lois would die if I ever mentioned to anyone what we'd done together, and I never would, but I could sense her acute inner discomfort as I said that.

"You just want to be different, to *pretend* to be different," Ketti said. "Bisexual sounds so, like, sophisticated."

"No, I just mean I'm confused. Seriously. I'm being honest. I have a closeness with all of you that I can't imagine having with a boy."

"That's not what it's all about," Andria said, "though I know what you mean. You, all of you, know me in some ways better than Hal . . . but it's just different. He makes me complete. It's not like: bingo, I have a man so I don't need all of you anymore. I'll need you all my life."

Lois was staring at her. She found Andria more intimidating than I did. "You sound like a mother sometimes," she said.

Andria made a face. "Whoa, talk about unkind blows!"

Lois looked around the room. "I just mean it's as if your life is all planned out. You just have to take the right steps. . . . I'm like Isabel. To me it all seems fuzzy and confusing."

Andria looked at all of us. "Once you're where I am, you'll see it's *not* like that. I could have met another Hal later in life, but I met him when I was twelve. I'm a compromiser. I'm not looking for some magical, 'this will bring everything together' thing."

"*I* want to live alone," Lois said. "I think I'd love that, not having to react and talk and, as you say, compromise."

"Spinster heaven," Ketti said dismissively. She could be cruel, just in not realizing how sensitive Lois was.

Lois flushed. "Spinster is an ugly word, *and* it's outdated. It's like I called you promiscuous."

Ketti sighed. "Touché. I take it back. . . . What I worry or wonder about, really, is whether it's sex I like or just the power it gives me over men. I mean, without the power . . . Do you really *like* it, Andria?"

"Yeah, I do. . . . I like everything about it. . . ."

"And you always really come?" Ketti pursued. "You don't fake it ever, *ever*?"

"Uh-uh," Andria said calmly. "I never have."

I was both fascinated and appalled. I wanted to know all this, but would never have had Ketti's bravado in asking. Taking my courage from her, I said, "Does that mean you always come, or when you don't you tell him?"

Andria blushed, which was rare for her. "I guess I just about always do," she said.

Ketti laughed. "Thank God you're a friend, or I'd really want to kill you."

"I always thought it would be like masturbating," Lois said hopefully.

"No," Ketti sat up. "Masturbating is a snap. Everyone knows how to please herself. But to get a guy to—"

"Ket, it's just that you haven't been with one guy long enough," Andria said. "Once you are, he'll get to know your body the way *you* know it."

"Would you sign a piece of paper that guarantees that in writing?" Ketti asked wryly.

"Sure." I could imagine Andria like one of those married women who write in to Ann Landers at eighty, saying her sex life with her husband is still as good as it ever was.

"So I guess this year it's Stuart," Ketti said. Suddenly she gave me an inquisitive glance. "Do I have your permission, Iz?"

"Why would you need that?" I asked coolly, my heart thumping.

"It's like you're his older sister. I could almost see you two as a couple, but in some weird way it would seem incestuous."

I stood up, stretching to cover my awkwardness. "Don't worry," I said. "We're just friends."

RESCUE

When I got interested in philosophy in my sophomore year, I had long talks with my father about whether one's fate was determined by genes, upbringing, the way one had been shaped by society, or just sheer chance. The way I met Stuart is a case in point. It was on the second or third day of nursery school, and we were both four years old. The teacher—whose name, Mrs. Darling, made her seem almost absurdly suited to her profession—allowed the parents to stay the first day or two. But by the third day (I know this because my mother told me much later) she told them they had to leave. "Leave quietly, unobtrusively," she advised. "By the time the children notice you're not here, they'll be busy with other things." Maybe that's good advice—I've never worked with small children, so I can't say—but the way I remember it, it was terrifying. I looked up and suddenly my mother wasn't there.

I can still see myself standing there—a scrawny little girl in tights and a smocked dress, with big ears sticking out like jug handles, wispy brownish hair, huge eyes, and a mouth half open, ready to emit an ear-piercing howl. At that moment Stuart passed by, grabbed my hand, and said, "Let's build something out of blocks."

He was a chunky little boy with greenish eyes and brown-blond hair falling into his face. I had no reason to assume another child was capable of the duplicity I already suspected from adults. I felt rescued, safe.

That was how our friendship started, and even though I soon made other friends, Lois most important, Stuart was the first. It was he who had stepped in and come between me and what seemed a fate worse than death. When, at lunchtime, I asked him where his mother was (I didn't dare ask about mine for fear of hearing some awful truth), he said, "She works, just like we play." He said this so matter-of-factly it made sense to me. Of course, Stuart's mother, Olive, *did* work—she had started silk-screening scarves and materials at home, which grew into a business—and mine didn't yet, but that didn't bother me. His explanation was convincing because of its simplicity: Children needed to play; mothers needed to work.

Our friendship might well have tapered off and vanished by first or second grade, when boys who played with girls were beginning to be considered suspect. Girls who played with boys could only be excused if they were "tomboys," good at sports, which I wasn't. In fact, if Stuart hadn't occasionally picked me when we were dividing ourselves into teams, I would always have been one of the last chosen.

But Stuart didn't pay any attention to the occasional teasing from the other boys. And then, the year we were both eight, it became even easier to be friends because Stuart and his mother took an apartment right on our floor, across the hall. It was my mother who mentioned the coming vacancy to Olive, and with typical alacrity Olive went to see the couple who were still living there that very night and called the real estate agent in the morning. I was never sure if my mother did this because she genuinely liked Olive and wanted her as a neighbor or just because she likes to befriend women she can feel superior to in some way. My mother felt superior to Olive because Olive was divorced and "forced" to have a profession and raise a son on her own, her French husband

10

having disappeared somewhere on the continent. And then, not only did Olive have lovers, she actually, when I was entering fifth grade, "stooped" (my mother's words) to marrying Chester, a man fifteen years her junior, an act my mother could only interpret as one of desperation. Needless to say, when two years later Chester had an affair with a young woman named Amber and Olive turned him out, my mother was flooded with triumph.

If I had been Olive, I might have detested my mother, but Olive never seemed to. Before, during, and after Chester she was always cheerful and friendly, ready to have me over for the weekend if my parents went away, grateful to my mother for having Stuart for meals. My mother was a good cook. *Joy of Cooking*, which her own mother had given her, was her bible, and she used it methodically, checking favorite recipes, starring certain ones. "S.F." meant "Sidney's favorite" (Sidney was my father); "I.F." was me; even Stuart, because he ate at our house so often, rated a sprinkling of stars. The fact is, Stuart loved food and eagerly ate anything you put in front of him. To my mother, used to my father's spastic colon and my appetite that mysteriously disappeared with anxiety, serving him was a pleasure. "This is great," Stuart would say, wolfing down a second, even a third helping. "Are you sure you have enough?"

"If that boy didn't have us, he would starve," my mother would comment grimly but happily when Stuart had gone home. "Thank God he has us."

"Thank God we have him," my father would say.

"Meaning?"

"Someone who can appreciate fine food, who has the appetite, the palate, the youthful vigor."

There was also the fact that my mother (and she made no secret about it) had always wanted a son. She had three sisters, and her father had died when she was a teenager. She liked what she called "the male presence"—it was never totally clear whether she meant that my father didn't supply enough of this, or that only having sons could have done the trick. Stuart and Olive seemed to have a friendship more than a mother-son relationship. They talked about sex, life, careers as though they were equals, something I envied and my mother thought "a great shame." But maybe my mother wasn't totally wrong. Maybe she did supply Stuart with a sense of a conventional home—my father being there physically, if not always emotionally or mentally—a little model of the nuclear family plunked right next door that he could visit the way some people visit model homes they have no intention of buying.

So Stuart and I grew up together like brother and sister. We played doctor, took baths together, looked at each other's bodies with the usual childhood curiosity. The thing I remember wondering about most was the purpose of belly buttons. We knew how they got there, we knew about umbilical cords; what we didn't understand was what role they played later on in producing babies. I was extremely ticklish, and Stuart used to tickle me with a peacock feather Olive kept in a large stone vase in their dining room. The second the feather touched my belly button, I started writhing on the floor in helpless laughter. Once I overheard Olive say that Chester was a lot of fun in bed, and I developed a private theory that they might have their own version of the peacock-feather game.

I had determined early on, at the age of five or six, that Stuart and I would eventually marry, but I refrained from sharing this information with him, confident that sooner or later he would come around to it himself. It made our high school years, in which he confided all his amorous possibilities to me, distinctly painful. I would listen calmly though, secure in the hope that someday he would come to his senses.

POCKETS OF
YEARNING

We lived near the public tennis courts at Central Park West and Ninety-third. Neither Stuart nor I was an especially good player, but we were, as he said, "consistent in our inconsistencies"—he had a strong serve but frequently double-faulted; I had a weak, blooping serve but got almost everything back. We never played sets. Instead we had invented a game that suited both our temperaments. We kept score, but we never added the game scores up. Sometimes Stuart would tease that ever since we had started playing tennis, when we were twelve, he had kept an inner tally in his head, and would tell me the result when we graduated from high school. I think we were pretty evenly matched.

This summer, the summer before our senior year, we hadn't played much. While I'd been doing tumor research with a young, slightly spacy junior scientist at the laboratory, Stuart had gone to Maine to teach tennis at an all-boys camp Chester had once gone to. He and Chester were still friends— or maybe they had always been more like friends than stepfather and stepson, with only a decade in age between them. Olive still kept in touch with Chester (who had immediately broken up with Amber), but she refused to get back together with him.

Our first game of the season took place the day after the "fearsome foursome" had met at our apartment. Stuart said his elbow had been bothering him, so we agreed to quit before the hour was up. We sat under a tree looking out at the courts.

"Is your elbow really bothering you?" I asked.

"Off and on. . . . Playing tennis six hours a day wasn't the greatest experience of my life. At least if it had been a coed camp, I could have had furtive thrills of coaching Lolita-like eleven-year-olds. These were just gung-ho obnoxious little brats."

"Wasn't there a girls' camp?" It seemed to me there nearly always was.

"Yeah, they had dances a couple of times." He looked offhand, then half smiled.

"Meaning what?" I felt like a hawk ready to dive.

"One kind of nice girl, Shelley, who had a boyfriend back home. We sort of half made out. She wasn't prudish, she just . . . And then, I don't know, I figured why set up something when you're not going to follow through?"

Stuart had lost his virginity at a similar camp last year. I bit the bullet when he described his sexual adventures, which he didn't do in a macho way. I think he genuinely assumed I'd be interested, and that I'd tell him my own adventures, if they ever occurred. "Did anything of interest happen at the lab?" he asked.

"I didn't cure cancer."

"I meant with guys."

"They were all a lot older."

"So?"

I feigned greater coolness than I felt, trying to imitate his tone. "Well, like you say, why start something if . . . I mean, no one was a soul mate, *or* an object of unrelenting lust."

He laughed and looked at me with that teasing, affection-ate expression. "Unrelenting lust hits Isabel Lear. I want a video of that."

"You'll be the first to know." I looked at him, trying to

14

decide if I would consider Stuart attractive if I could back off enough for that kind of detachment. He'd grown taller—five feet eight—he didn't have jug ears, or crooked teeth or bad skin. He was still a bit on the chunky side, with hair that had darkened to plain brown and stood up in peculiar cowlicks and curls. A Huck Finn. He still loved to eat, and I could imagine him being a little too fat in middle age.

"What's wrong?" he said, picking up, as he often did, on my thoughts. "I didn't gain one pound over the summer. I just weighed myself this morning. It wasn't willpower, admittedly, just rotten food."

"You look fine."

"I don't want to be too much of a sex object and cause all our female classmates to run amok. Have you seen anyone?"

"The 'fearsome foursome' came over yesterday."

"And—no, let me guess. Andria and Hal exchanged fifty-five three-page, single-spaced letters, and she knit him eight more blue scarves. Ketti seduced the father of the kids she was baby-sitting on Fire Island. Lois saw three dozen old movies at the Regency and had erotic dreams about Jimmy Stewart."

"You're so bitchy." Actually, I liked the way Stuart was interested in what all of us were doing.

"Look, if I were your typical red-blooded American male, you'd have no use for me. It's just because my female side is so overdeveloped that you tolerate my company."

On the one hand, Stuart and I told each other everything. On the other hand, we didn't. I had never told him about what Lois and I had done together, neither the acts themselves nor the thoughts and feelings leading up to them. Nor did we ever discuss the peacock-feather period of our relationship, except obliquely when Stuart would try to tickle me, or wave the feather menacingly in my direction if I was giving him a hard time. I'm not so sure what he didn't tell me, but I assume there were the same blanks. "I went to the movies with Chester a couple of times," I said.

He started. "I thought older men were a taboo. He's twenty-six!"

"It's like you and me. We're pals. He wants someone to mope to about Olive, someone who knows her."

Stuart sat up impatiently. "That's such bullshit."

"I think he's sincere."

"The guy thinks with his prick. You have these insanely high ideals about men, and then you fall for that kind of unbelievable crap."

"Stu, hey! Chill, okay? You've always said you *liked* him—"

"As a pal, as a quasi sibling. I think of him as a younger brother, if you want to know."

"So do I. . . . And I think he still loves Olive, and I also think she has no intention of taking him back, and she shouldn't."

Stuart seemed temporarily mollified. Then his face darkened. "There's a new cloud, or one could say male presence, on the horizon. Have you met him?"

I shook my head. I had gone over to talk to Olive a few times over the summer, but she'd always been alone. "Who is he?"

"Another loser, to be viciously blunt. He's forty-eight, and just getting his doctorate in clinical psychology—one of those sixties leftovers. I mean, a gold chain? A pony-tail?"

"Is it serious?" I always thought of Olive as the platonic ideal of the type Stuart was describing. She had had waist-length black hair which she had cut to shoulder length when she'd turned forty a year ago. There was still something not only youthful but carefree, intense, and appealing about her. She and Chester had never seemed to me an ill-matched couple, despite the age difference. But unlike Chester, who was still "finding himself," Olive had a profession, earned a decent living, wasn't just writing unpublishable poetry or walking barefoot in the rain.

Stuart shrugged.

"She's entitled to her own life," I said, defending her. "You'll be gone soon. . . ."

He was lying on his back, squinting up at the trees. "Why doesn't she get someone solid . . . like your father?"

16

I stared at him in disbelief. "You're kidding. My *father*? He's a hundred years older than her mentally. Leaving aside my mother—no, but that's it. Can you picture someone who chose my mother by his own free will making someone like Olive happy in bed?"

"Yeah, well . . . But your father can probably still get it up, occasionally, can't he?"

"I haven't tallied their rate of intercourse lately." Actually, I had always assumed my parents had no sex life, because they kept such different hours: My mother was asleep by eleven every night, my father was a night owl who rarely went to bed before one or two.

"Olive claims that what she learned from Chester was that being an earth mother wasn't her thing, but that's exactly what she's doing with this Jerry character," Stuart said heatedly. "She starts feeding them these huge, nutritious meals, finds them apartments, falls into bed with them . . . *then* she complains they're too dependent on her." He wrinkled his nose. Stuart had a big nose, which had he been a girl he might have had carved down by some expert, expensive surgeon, but I was glad he'd never even considered it. He jokingly claimed that non-Jewish girls found it sexy, that it was an erogenous zone.

"We should trade mothers," I said. I'd had that fantasy as far back as I could remember.

"No, you're what you are because you've had the conventional thing to rebel against. You can *be* it, reject it. I have to start from scratch." He looked woebegone.

"Personally I don't think having a sexy, warm, intelligent, financially successful mother is *such* a burden," I said wryly. My mother, who had stayed home when I was younger, now had a job at an institute concerned with the restoration of old buildings in New York. It had started as a volunteer job, but now she was paid, and it was unfair of me to still consider it not a "real job." But administration seemed to me something my mother did because she had a flair for it—not the total passion that Olive had for her work.

Stuart shook his head. "It *is* a burden! Look at the pros-

17

pects for me. I'll probably marry an older woman, so as to continue my relationship with Ol—something like the Chester thing. Then I'll be unfaithful with some total jerk, like Amber, break this poor devoted woman's heart . . . but what can I do? *She'll* be gray haired, she'll begin looking like Ol, the oedipal implications will be overwhelming. I'll be trapped, helpless. . . ."

Stuart wanted to be a shrink. In fact, he'd gone to one when he was younger and having horrible nightmares, and he had loved it. He confessed later that he pretended to have nightmares long after they had actually stopped, just because he and Dr. Burns, a crisp, thoughtful woman in her thirties, had such good rap sessions. "I *want* to marry a younger man," I said. "I think your mother has the right idea. I mean, look at my father! He isn't fifty yet, and he acts like he's eighty, creeping around, wearing bifocals, moaning about all his aches and pains. I feel like he's my grandfather at times."

"Well, go to Olive," Stuart said. "She'll give you lessons. Frankly, I think the secret is her spaghetti carbonara."

"*My* mother's a good cook, and I don't see any younger men drooling over her."

"How about me?" Stuart said.

"You like her cooking, you're not lusting after her in secret."

"True," he admitted. When he smiled in that warm, affectionate, teasing way, a pang would go through me. I was direly ashamed of my fantasies about Stuart, infinitely more than of the fact that Lois and I had once or twice furtively caressed each other's bodies. I never thought about Lois at night, alone in the dark, the way I did about Stuart. If I had trouble falling asleep, I would take out one of my standard Stuart fantasies and start it unreeling, like some favorite movie. In one, already outdated, he would ask me, as a favor, if I would be willing to have sex with him to relieve him of his virginity. I would comply, under the pretense that it was an act of pure friendship. Once Stuart had actually lost his virginity, I reversed it. In the

18

new version he came to me and said, if I wanted, he would be willing to break me in for the same motives, just so I wouldn't have to go off to college a virgin. In fact, I felt Stuart would almost have been willing to do that, if I had asked, but woven into our seemingly no-holds-barred, sister-brother closeness were these secret pockets of yearning and lust that I never revealed.

He stood up. "You didn't tell me the gossip," he said as we were striding past the benches. "Who's Ketti gunning for this year?"

"You," I blurted out.

To my alarm, he blushed. "God, what have I done to deserve that? She must be desperate."

"Andria thought you'd be a good couple. She said—let me see if I can quote this accurately—that Ketti was kooky and fun loving, and that you were seemingly put together, but with underpinnings of confusion."

He shuddered. "Jesus, the four of you are like witches. Did you stick a little pin in some voodoo doll? . . . No, it's horribly accurate. The male psyche dissected mercilessly by four sharp-eyed females."

"Ketti was afraid you'd be too easy, that she could make you her helpless slave with a minimum of trouble." I always did this. My seeming frankness had the inner motive of preventing what I dreaded would happen.

"Boy, she's right, there! I'm the world's greatest softie with women. But what have I done to deserve being Ketti's helpless slave my senior year? When does it start? Do I fall limply at her feet the first day of school? Or will she appear at midnight in a trench coat with nothing underneath, and an iced bottle of champagne?"

"We didn't plan strategy."

"We! So every little perverse thing Ketti and I do will be plotted in advance and reported back to Central Headquarters?" He wrinkled his nose. "I don't know if I can take that, all of you cackling and drooling over my sex life."

I made a mock cackle. "Once you're doing it, you'll

19

shut up about it. That's how it was with Andria and Hal.''

He gave me a serious glance. "I never tell anyone anything, except you . . . and I never will.''

"Thanks." But there were many moments that year when I wished Stuart hadn't been as faithful in this as he promised.

HEART TO HEART

When I got out of the shower after our tennis game, there was a message on the answering machine that Chester had called. Still wrapped in the big bath towel, I called him back and told him Stuart was home from camp. "Great! How about the two of you coming over? I'll treat you to dinner. . . . Bring Olive, if she doesn't have anything better to do."

I gathered Chester, like me, didn't know about Olive's new boyfriend, Jerry. "I'll ask them," I promised. I didn't agree with Stuart about Chester. It seemed to me Chester's love for Olive was the only genuine adult version of sex and romance I had come across outside books and the movies. I felt Chester was really repentant. I believed his story, that Amber had seemed to him just a poor kid down on her luck in the big city, that he had felt protective of her, that eventually "one thing had led to another." Amber had a boyfriend back home whom she intended to marry. Because their brief romp had been to Chester so innocent, almost an act of charity, he hadn't bothered to conceal it—which would, he claimed, have been "easier than pie." He had been appalled

21

that Olive couldn't see it "the way it had really been," and had pitched him out so unceremoniously.

That had been four years ago. Maybe he hadn't been celibate for four years, but he had never stopped talking about Olive. I couldn't remember one conversation when he hadn't referred to her, asked about her, begged me to intervene on his behalf.

I didn't mind being a go-between. I saw Olive as sexually free but also in need of tender devotion. I wanted her to go off into the sunset with someone. "Chester wonders if we feel like coming over tonight," I told Stuart on the phone. "Olive too, if she's free."

He groaned. "Olive if she's free! . . . She *isn't* free, she isn't even here, and if she were, I wouldn't dignify that invitation by asking her."

"Well, *I* might go," I said. "Why not?"

"I told you! The guy's twenty-six! What is this—some desperate passion to get laid by the first day of school?"

Despite myself, I started giggling. "Stu, seriously, Chester has never so much as laid a hand on me."

"A foot?"

"Not even a big toe. . . . I'm just the go-between."

"And you don't mind being used that way? That's so sick, Iz. Where's your sense of pride?"

"I'm not being used. I like him. We have fun together. But if you don't want to come, fine."

"I'll come, but only to protect you. You're such a fucking innocent. This guy could have you in bed, and you'd be too absorbed watching some X-rated video to know how you got there."

"Have you showered?"

"I have—I've just been admiring my body in the full-length mirror. I'm in really great shape. Ketti isn't as much of a fool as I thought. She has a treat in store, if she can get to me before I munch myself back into my usual tubbiness."

After hanging up I let the towel drop and looked at myself naked in the hall mirror. There was nothing conspicuously wrong with my body, but it looked unused, like those books

22

in libraries that they put in plastic wrappers, that no one checks out.

We met at one of Chester's favorite Indian restaurants. Chester grinned when he saw Stuart and gave him a hug. "You look great!" he said. "Doesn't he, Iz? They must have worked you to death."

Stuart just shrugged sheepishly.

"All those cute little teenage girls wanting help with their backhand," Chester pursued. "I bet you had a busy summer."

"Sorry, Chester. It was an all-boys camp, remember?" Stuart said.

"No girls' camp anymore across the lake? Poor fellow. Well, once you get back to school, you'll have your pick."

"I've been spoken for," Stuart said, relaxing. "Isabel tells me that her friend Ketti is planning a major assault on my virtue. I, of course, shall stand firm."

Chester frowned. "Which one is Ketti?" He knew about the "fearsome foursome," had met and flirted with all of us, made us feel grown-up and sexy, even when we were as undeveloped as new potatoes.

"Blondish, skinny, with devilish green eyes," Stuart said.

Chester ordered curry for us all. He was wearing a peculiar greenish tunic, belted, and baggy gray slacks. "But she is the promiscuous one, right? And what about AIDS? Stuart, don't, it's not worth it—"

"Promiscuous!" Stuart raised his eyebrows, meaning Chester was in no position to make such a remark. "She's been around a little. . . . How many, Iz? You probably know exactly."

Chester always looked embarrassed when Stuart horsed around like that with me. "But is it true deep attraction?" he pursued. "Or is it just—"

"Lust," Stuart said. "It's one of those animal things that can't be explained, that she'll regret all her life if she doesn't give in to it."

Chester sighed. "You are so young, both of you. . . . This is the year to get ready for college, to think about important

23

things, not to waste yourself or jeopardize your entire future. You and Isabel have each other as companions. Later, when you're ready, you can find the other, the special thing. Believe me, it comes once in a lifetime, that's all."

"That often?" Stuart said, quoting from *An American in Paris*. He and I quoted like that from our favorite movies all the time.

Chester put his arm around Stuart. "When you're young, you can pretend to be cynical. At my age, you know the difference. You feel it—here." He pointed somewhere in the area of his chest.

"In your upper thorax?" Stuart said. "Have you had that checked by a doctor?"

But Chester, as always, refused to rise to the bait. "When you feel it, Stuart, you'll stop regarding it as a joke."

"God, I hope not," Stuart said. "You mean that's the first sign of true love? Losing your sense of humor?"

Chester looked contemplative. "You'll be vulnerable, less defensive. Don't you agree, Isabel?"

"I—" I began, but Stuart interrupted.

"I'm as vulnerable as a newborn kitten! Ketti already is planning on making me her slave. Iz told me. She thinks I'll be such an easy lay, I may not even be worth bothering with. Well, I'll show her. I'll put up a struggle, a real fight. She'll have to beg, to plead." He looked at me keenly. "What was that you said once about her? Is she frigid, or what?"

I blushed. "Stu, come on, this is all . . . secrets."

"Secrets!" He guffawed. "They sit there and they analyze their boyfriends, how good they are in bed, their psychological problems. . . . I'm not asking out of any seedy prurient interest. I just want to know how to proceed. Get out the old peacock feather—that's surefire."

Chester looked puzzled. "Olive loves peacock feathers," he said wistfully.

Stuart winked at me. "Right."

Chester was looking from one of us to the other. "I don't know if I should mention this," he said slowly. "I may be wrong—it's a very small thing—but one night I dropped over and a man was there, and I had the feeling—there was some-

24

thing in his manner toward her, perhaps because he knew about me, something proprietary. . . . You know that kind of man?''

''Which kind?'' Stuart asked with seeming innocence.

''The empty-headed macho kind,'' Chester said with fierce contempt, ''who feels he must flaunt his— The point is, this man is not worthy of Olive. I am not speaking from sexual jealousy. I am speaking as her friend, because to me that is what she will always be, no matter what.''

Stuart sighed. ''Well, you may be right, but I think it's too late.''

Chester looked horror-struck. ''Late? In what way?''

''Did the guy have a gold chain? A beard?''

''Yes, yes . . . Imagine, a gold chain!'' He wrinkled his nose in distaste. Given Chester's general appearance and style of dressing, it was hard to know why a gold chain would be so terrible.

''Jerry,'' Stuart said. ''That's his name. Yeah, he's semi-moved in. When I came back from camp, the first sight that greeted me was him in his pajamas, fighting for the C section of the *Times*.''

''And since then?''

''That was yesterday.''

Chester looked relieved. ''Then it's not too late. . . . They're not deeply involved?''

''I haven't had a chance to play the grand inquisitor,'' Stuart said. ''She did look a little dewy-eyed and sparkly, but nothing too extreme.''

Chester grabbed my hands. ''Isabel, you love Olive, don't you?''

''Of course.''

''Perhaps you can talk to her, heart to heart, as they say. She would be throwing herself away. It pains me to think of that possibility.'' He looked in genuine pain.

I felt embarrassed. ''But I'm just a kid, Chester. I mean, I don't know anything about those things. Really.''

Again he grabbed my hands. ''You're a woman,'' he said. ''You were born knowing.''

''I think Iz is right,'' Stuart put in. ''If Ol wants to make a fool of herself over some jerk, she'll do it. It won't be the first time.''

''What is beautiful about Olive is her innocence,'' Chester said. ''She will never lose that. People thought I was so much younger than her, but they were wrong. In spirit I was old, cynical, dried up, and Olive was young, fresh.''

''Why're we worrying about Ol?'' Stuart said. ''She'll do okay. She knows men, maybe not wisely, but well. Some are just for fun, for the moment. . . . You know who we *should* be worried about?''

''Who?'' Chester asked.

Stuart pointed to me. ''This one. She's the real innocent, untouched, unspoiled—''

I kicked him sharply under the table. ''Shut up, Stu.''

''Isabel has more sense than any of us,'' Chester said. ''When she makes her choice, it will be for life. That I have no doubt about.''

''But till then?''

''Till then she will do as her inclinations allow her.'' He looked grave. ''Sometimes you are unthinking and rude, Stuart.''

''I'm a man,'' he said. ''What can I do?'' He turned to me. ''Why do women like men? It really amazes me. Emotionally we're cretins.''

''Not all of us,'' Chester said.

''Yeah, all of us,'' Stuart said belligerently. ''You most of all. Even more than me. At least I have the glaze of self-knowledge, without which I'd be . . .''

Chester smiled at him indulgently. ''I think I'll put the two of you in a cab,'' he said. He paid and we let him. After all, he'd invited us.

I gave the cabdriver our address. Stuart leaned against me. ''I was a jerk, right?''

''Totally. You bait him, you humiliate me. Sometimes I hate you!'' I was surprised at my intensity.

''Sometimes I hate myself,'' Stuart said. He took my hand and wove our fingers together. ''But I'm a guy. Guys are fools.''

''That's so stupid!'' I said. ''That's such an excuse.''

"*You're* always saying it. Men this, men that . . ."

"But I *mean* it. You're just blathering on out of self-pity, or God knows what. And why do you act like such a beast with Chester? He loves Olive, and you don't know *anything* about what that's like! You know *nothing*!"

Stuart roused himself. "He loved her so much he was unfaithful to her with the first beddable thing with knockers that crossed his path?"

"How about forgiveness? How about human charity? You're going to be faithful all your life, to whomever you marry?"

"Yes," Stuart said angrily. "I damn well am—all the rest is shit."

IMAGINARY CHILDREN

Mr. O'Reilly was my favorite teacher at Whitman. I met with him the first day of school to plan my senior project. He was gay. Maybe it's partly generational, but I think in his case character plays as large a role in keeping him walled in, like Aïda in her tomb. He was quite formal and had a slightly English manner, wearing a suit and tie to school, for instance, whereas half the male teachers wore denim shirts rolled to their elbows, and chinos. He was the first person to read my poetry and take it at all seriously. I was thirteen then, and he sighed wryly and said, "I fear you have a calling. But let's not be drastic. It may be a passing phase."

Knowing I had worked at the lab all summer, he was now suggesting the idea of combining poems on scientific subjects with short essays or descriptions of what it had been like working there. "I did write a few poems," I said. "How many do you think would be needed?"

"Why don't you let it evolve and bring them in to me from time to time? The ratio of prose to poetry isn't important. I just thought it would be an interesting way of approaching the material."

"I'll try."

"You sound hesitant." He had pale-blue eyes, white-sand hair, and an almost uncanny sensitivity about my moods.

"It's just, it's so much like what my father has been trying to do for years."

"Does he write poetry?" Mr. O'Reilly looked startled. "Sidney, the ophthalmologist? How fascinating!"

"No, not poetry," I reassured him. "Essays on scientific topics. Some have gotten published, but they're just, well, horribly dry."

Mr. O'Reilly smiled. "One would imagine."

"His best friend always says, 'Give it more juice, Sid.' But I guess he can't."

"Few of us can," Mr. O'Reilly said. "Even those who fancied they *had* juice to begin with. . . . But tell me, Isabel, how do you feel now about your future? Does a life devoted to research tempt you?"

I hated to disappoint him. If Olive was my spiritual mother, Mr. O'Reilly was my spiritual father, though they would have been rather an odd connubial combination. "I just don't think so. . . . It's totally abstract. I think I need something more practical."

"Public health, perhaps?"

"Maybe . . . but medicine sounds terribly macho to me, and then people dying, at least some of the time . . . I don't know about that."

"Oh, of course not medicine," Mr. O'Reilly said. "Nothing *that* practical. It's just, well, here I'm doing what I feel teachers should be *fired* for doing, but I'd like to see you make a decision that would use your best energies, even ones that seem at odds with each other, as I, quite definitely, didn't."

Mr. O'Reilly had once confessed to me that he had had a beautiful voice in his youth and wanted to be an opera singer, but that he had used it "profligately," and that by the time he was in his twenties, "the bloom was gone."

"I'd like something that would allow me time to write," I said.

"Yes, there's the rub," he said. "You don't want to go

into anything *too* directly connected, like publishing. And then you don't want to be one of us."

"You mean go into teaching?"

"High school teaching especially. It's like *The Picture of Dorian Gray*, only it happens overnight instead of taking years. One day you walk into this building bright, bushy tailed, idealistic, and the next week, *two* if you're lucky, you have an ulcer, you start twitching when you see teenagers on the subway, you can't even hear yourself lecture."

"*You're* not like that," I said, though I didn't think he was begging for compliments.

"Dry rot of the soul," Mr. O'Reilly said. "It invades, but it doesn't always kill every cell. And do you know why?"

I shook my head.

"This is fanciful, you will indulge me, it's that now and again one finds certain imaginary children, not of one's loins, but of one's soul, and they sustain the inner spark. . . . You, a few others . . ."

I blushed. "Thank you."

He looked dreamy, lost in thought. "Real children of all ages terrify me. This is different."

I smiled. "They terrify me too."

"Then don't have them. Don't feel forced to have them. Women are more at risk in these matters than men. Don't become a beast of burden to some hopeless man, Isabel. I don't mean celibacy, or even avoiding marriage. But be as selfish as your nature will allow you to be. Life traps all of us so very cunningly. Be wary."

"I will."

The few times my mother had met Mr. O'Reilly, grateful as she was to him for "encouraging" me, she hadn't altogether trusted him. "I don't mind that he's gay," she said, and I was surprised she knew—she struck me as very unobservant. "But he's not a real poet. How can he know what he's talking about? And he's so prissy. It was eighty-nine degrees in his office, and he wore a tie!"

Usually my mother liked men who looked dapper and well dressed, but I knew what she meant. Mr. O'Reilly seemed encased, ill at ease, even in the uniform he'd chosen for himself. I stopped trying to defend him, just as I stopped trying to defend Olive. They were among my secret loves, and I wanted to protect them both from my mother's withering sarcasm.

I saw Lois in the hall just before lunch and we compared notes. "Physics will be brutish," she said, sighing.

"I don't get why you're not taking geology." Lois was hopeless at science.

"Daddy thinks I should push myself. He says physics has inner beauty, once you get past the formulas."

"Didn't he say that about geometry?"

Lois's father, a widower, was an editor. Her mother had died when we were in junior high. "So I get a C," she said, shrugging. "I'll get into Mount Holyoke because Mom went there. It's different for you. You're aiming higher."

It wasn't, in fact, all that different. My father had gone to Princeton and kept making sly little hints about taking me to meet his friend, the dean. My mother had gone to the University of Wisconsin, and thought Princeton was elitist. I was determined to make up my own mind. Princeton seemed uncomfortably close to home. I had fantasies of Reed in Oregon, which I had sensibly kept to myself.

"Meet me after school?" Lois asked.

"Sure." We'd been doing this since first grade, going to Lois's house or mine. It would seem strange next year to see each other only during vacation.

After our last class Lois and I had ice-cream sodas—my favorite, all coffee; her favorite, vanilla with chocolate ice cream. Then we stopped off at the grocery store to get food for dinner. Lois's father, Miller, liked to boast that he never went near the kitchen. Lois did all the cooking, but he did all the housework, so it wasn't as sexist as it sounded. Like my father, he was precise and neat, but I had never in my life seen my father vacuuming, or polishing windows, or dusting. "I love it," Miller claimed. "I've found my calling. It's the perfect way to unwind after a long day at the office."

"Did you see Ketti playing up to Stuart?" Lois asked as we left the store.

"No." Involuntarily my heart sank. "When?"

"Oh, I forget. Just a bit of the old head-to-one-side, mischievous-smile thing. I wonder how long it will take."

"A month," I suggested.

"That long?"

"Long?" I was horrified. I'd made it go quick, hoping she'd say not before Christmas."

Lois shifted her bundle to the other arm. "Well, neither of them are virgins, and . . . But you're right. Maybe she'll change her mind. I don't really think he's her type."

I wished Lois hadn't made it seem it was all up to Ketti. "In what way?"

"Well, Stuart's so . . . introspective, really, despite joking around a lot. I think he needs someone he can really talk to—like what he has with you, only with romance thrown in."

It was a tribute to my deep need for privacy that I had never even hinted to Lois what I felt about Stuart. "I think he needs romance," I said. "And it wouldn't be forever, just for this year."

"They *could* end up engaged, like Andria and Hal," Lois said bluntly, completely changing tack.

My heart was thudding in that uncomfortable way again. "I thought you said—"

"Oh, what do I know?" Lois said disparagingly. "I mean, seriously. Maybe men want to be helpless slaves . . . or the other way around. Maybe the friendship-plus-romance thing is a farce."

For some reason I had a quick vision of Stuart naked, turning and looking at me slavishly. "Should I make Gregory Arrington my helpless slave?" I said, to turn off these thoughts.

We had reached the lobby of Lois's apartment building. As the elevator door closed, Lois said vehemently, "I thought that was so cruel of Andria. Gregory's just a fool, a drip. . . . Why does everyone have to be tied up in neat little couples? God, when I think of being connected that way, at our age, I feel *sick*. She can't understand that we regard *ourselves* as the lucky ones."

"Right," I said halfheartedly. "I felt that way when Ketti

called it spinster heaven when you said you wanted to live alone.''

"They don't get it," Lois said. "They just assume everyone wants what *they* have—either some neat, suffocating little marriage, or just fucking guys for a thrill. But what's ironical is Ketti claims she doesn't even get orgasms. So what's the point?''

"Search me.'' We went into Lois's apartment. Her father, a university press editor who worked at home one day a week, was in the living room with a manuscript on his lap. He waved when he saw me.

"Welcome!'' he called out. "Staying for supper?''

"I'd love to.'' I hadn't seen Miller all summer, since Lois had been in Boston, living with her cousin and working at a day-care center. Although he was taller and beefier, I thought of Miller as a generic version of my father—he had the same dry wit, seeming detachment, and lack of need for other people. Lois said that on the day her mother died, he went to the office and never told anyone. He never "dated" or saw women, and had informed friends that if they ever tried to fix him up, he would sever the friendship on the spot. He never seemed to think it odd that Lois's social life was nonexistent.

I helped Lois put the groceries away.

"Your parents were always so happy," I said impulsively. "Mine seem content in being miserable. They just love it.''

Lois poured herself some juice. "I don't think they are miserable," she said softly. "Some people don't like to show what they really feel, about romantic things, I mean. It's too painful.'' She blushed, and I felt confused, not knowing if she was talking about us, too.

NAPS

By October it seemed as though the infamous Jerry, as Stuart called him, had settled in for the long haul. Stuart claimed it was just economic necessity. "He lives in this real fleabag," he said. "Not just fleas, though. Water bugs the size of your foot. He claims he doesn't mind, that things of the spirit are what count. Those are the guys to look out for. If he just said: 'Hell, I've lucked into a terrific lady with a great apartment who cooks like a dream, and has this intelligent, helpful son,' *then* I'd believe him."

"Olive seems happy," I said lamely.

Stuart shrugged. "I'm almost desperate enough to start pleading Chester's cause. . . . I think she ought to try celibacy for a change. They say it does wonders for the complexion."

"I guess that's why my skin's so great."

He squeezed my arm. "You've always had great skin. Especially inside your belly button." We were at the hallway outside our two apartments. My father had put up a Persian print, and Olive had hung one of her silk-screened prints, which swayed when the elevator door opened. "Have dinner with us," he said impulsively. "It's your mother's night at the Institute, and your father's going to a movie with a friend."

"How do you know?"

"I have my spies working. . . . And luck is with us. I think Gold Chain's ex-wife is in town, so we'll have the pleasure of his noncompany while we eat."

Jerry was, in fact, on his way out as we entered the apartment. He kissed me on both cheeks, as he always did, and pretended to look crushed. "I've got to go. Tell Olive I bought everything she asked for. . . . Ciao, Stu."

When he was out of sight, Stuart shuddered. "Ciao!"

"At least he's helping with the cooking," I pointed out.

"The grocery shopping, you mean. And he eats like it was going out of style. If he didn't jog six miles a day, he'd be in big trouble." He squeezed his stomach. "Tell me honestly, am I reverting to the way I looked before the summer?"

"You look fine. . . . Your tan has faded a little."

"I wonder if I'm coming down with something. I feel really zapped. Maybe I'll nap for a while. Want to? Or don't you do that anymore?"

When we were little, our mothers used to let us nap together, so that only one of them had to be on duty at a time. I sucked my thumb, Stuart had his bear, Hoffman. We had a ritual of lying back to back, our behinds touching, me facing the window, Stuart facing the wall. Even after we officially gave up naps, we would sometimes do it, always in that same position, though Hoffman had been retired and I no longer sucked my thumb. "Sure." I was always afraid if I acted even slightly hesitant, Stuart would think something had changed, that there was more than just the comfort of habit and physical warmth in our lying side by side—or back to back.

But it still worked. Either I was sleepier than I'd known or I wanted to escape thinking about the connotations of sharing a bed with Stuart, but I fell asleep in a matter of minutes. When I woke up and turned around, Stuart was lying on his back, his knees up, his eyes open. "This could look incriminating," he said.

"To whom?" Olive was totally relaxed about things like that; I was sure she wouldn't have cared if we had been lovers.

"True. Everything is in the mind of the beholder." The phone rang, and he reached over to pick it up. "Oh hi, Ket. . . . No, Isabel and I are just lying here, taking a nap." He chuckled. "Right, you've got it." As they continued chatting, I got off the bed, slipped back into my sneakers, and left the room. There was something so awful about it, the way he referred to us in that joking way, the way Ketti must have responded, as though big deal, good old Iz, the ultimate noncontender. That was one of Ketti's favorite phrases: "She's a noncontender." She had never used it to describe any of us, but that was probably just out of politeness.

I was setting the table, carefully arranging knives and forks and spoons, when Stuart ambled in. "Sorry, I forgot she'd said she'd call."

"I was up anyway." I looked at him quickly. "Are you ensnared yet?"

"Only physically," he said, and grinned. Then added, "Not really. Fooling around. I think that's Ketti's strong suit, and it has much to recommend it."

"Right." I yawned.

"Ketti thinks you need someone," he said. "I squelched the Gregory Arrington idea as being too pathetic to even contemplate."

"Squelch the whole thing," I snapped. "It's none of Ketti's fucking business! She and Andria think everyone has to be roped off into tidy little couples, or just . . ." I heard my own voice echoing Lois.

"I know," Stuart agreed. "I hate that. There's something catty about Ketti, something not quite aboveboard. But then, who am I to talk? I'm always criticizing everyone."

"Why bother with her, then?" I folded the paper napkins in two.

He smiled. "I'm flattered, it feels good, no one's being

36

hurt. And I like the fact that Ketti's so matter-of-fact about sex. She's not like most girls that way. You don't get the feeling she's hoping to get you to fall in love with her, to snare you.''

"Hah!''

Stuart looked surprised. ''Oh, you mean the helpless-slave thing? No, I meant big-time romance, like Andria and Hal, where they're already picking the names for their kids, and what street to live on when they buy their first co-op. Can you believe this? Hal came up to me today and said, 'How do you like Sean?' I said, 'Who's he?' He said, 'Andria and I can't decide which would be better, Sean or Kevin, for our first.' '' He whistled. ''I don't know, that's a little hard to get a handle on. . . . It's like they've been married forty years already.''

I was still thinking of our lying in bed, behinds touching, and wondering if sex could be just a more intense version of that. Then I thought of my parents, who slept in separate beds, and Olive, whose bed was enormous. Stuart waved a hand in front of my face. ''Hey, anybody home?''

"I was just thinking about beds,'' I said dreamily.

''As articles of furniture, or as places where people perform certain acts?''

"I was thinking of single versus double beds.''

"One bed,'' Stuart said, ''definitely.''

Olive came home at seven. Stuart and I had fixed everything, even put the bread in to be warmed. She was wearing the coat I loved, a cloak really, of a million different colors that somehow didn't clash but whirled around her. She set down her parcels, sniffed, and said, ''Did you really get everything ready? How great! I told Jerry to pick up a few things. He can't be here for dinner because his ex-wife—''

''We met him,'' Stuart said, ''on our way in.''

Olive never seemed surprised when I was there for dinner—never asked why, or if I had checked with my mother. She had been like that even when I was six. My mother always told Stuart, ''Be sure and check if it's all right with your mother, dear. We don't want to discommode her.''

Olive was wearing a turquoise-blue top and slacks, her

37

usual sandals, and an earring in one ear, a cluster of opals that caught and reflected the light. She poured us all wine, as she always did.

"I'll have a beer," Stuart said, getting up to get it.

"With shrimp?" Olive look horrified. "How can I have raised a child with such plebeian tastes?"

"The other side of the family?" Stuart suggested.

"Marcel's French!" Olive said. "He was drinking wine in his baby bottle! You're just trying to be perverse to annoy me. Or maybe it's some macho phase, denim shirts and cowboy boots next."

"Isabel would disown me," Stuart said, smiling at me.

"You have to hand it to Jerry, Stuart, really you do," Olive said, spearing a shrimp.

"What do I have to hand to him?"

She paused a moment, swallowing her wine. "No, look, I know you think he's selfish, self-absorbed, what have you, but look at the way he treats his ex-wife, Peggy. Whenever she's truly down and out, he comes to her rescue. . . . He's even letting her stay at his place for as long as she wants, till she can get her act together."

"Maybe she can talk to the water bugs," Stuart said.

Olive sighed ruefully. "Why is he like this?" she appealed to me.

"He's a tease," I said.

"Me?" Stuart said. "I?"

"Plus, he's jealous," I went on mercilessly. "*You* have someone, he doesn't."

"This is absurd," Stuart said. "Here I am, exerting infinite superhuman control when this sex fiend whom Isabel sicced on me calls me every night, tries to get me to show her parts of my body that are too private even to mention . . . and she says I have nobody."

"Ketti?" Olive said dismissively. "She's not worth an ounce of your attention."

"How do you know?" Stuart said. "Maybe she's great in bed."

"Is she?" we fired back simultaneously.

38

Stuart laughed. "Whoa, wait a sec. . . . I can barely handle one of you at a time."

It felt so good not only being able to joke about this but to have an ally. "Word has it," I said, helping myself to more shrimp, "that she's semifrigid."

"That's it!" Stuart said. "I've had the air conditioning on too high. She did look a little semifrigid, now that you mention it."

Olive was picking at her salad. "You haven't answered our question."

"You two think I'm such an easy lay," Stuart said. "I just topple into bed with the nearest available whoever. I happen to have great powers of discrimination. This is my senior year. I want to get into a good college. Far be it from me to waste valuable time on anyone who wouldn't savor the experience to the hilt. . . . And who the fuck are either of *you* to talk?" He looked genuinely angry.

Olive and I looked at each other. "We know you inside out," Olive said. "Why *shouldn't* we offer advice?"

He turned to her. "You? Two husbands? One half-assed lover who's a perpetual student with a schizy wife 'thinking about' getting a doctorate in archaeology? Countless—"

Olive put her hand over his mouth. "Countless nothing! I can count every one of them. And I'm of age. I know what I'm doing, while I'm doing it."

"That's worse," Stuart said. "You—"

"You know something about all these men, and there are as many things you *don't* know," Olive said, flushing. Sometimes the intensity of their battles seemed to have an amorous quality.

"And who is Isabel to talk?" Stuart went on angrily. "The great observer who never risks one iota of her precious body or soul on any mere mortal. Let those who have fought on the front lines talk about battle scars."

Olive rolled her eyes. "Have you been at Jerry's pot? If so, he'll skin you alive. It's worth a fortune."

"Haven't gone near it," Stuart said. "Only gazed at it

39

lovingly." He was munching on a large hunk of French bread.

I, of course, had been cut to the quick by his remarks about me. "I'm not an observer," I said bitterly. "That's too generous. I'm a noncontender." To Olive I explained, "That's what Ketti calls someone who isn't worth even dismissing."

"She sounds like an all-out bitch," Olive said.

"Anyway," Stuart said to me, "you're wrong. Ketti's in awe of you. She says she has been ever since she came to Whitman. She was so flattered when the three of you let her be in your inner circle, it was the high point of her life."

I knew that was true. Andria had always had that rock-solid maternal competence that made her help children her own age when they were sick, or feeling out of it, and Lois and I had our quiet, secret little world. But Ketti, because she was pretty, and skinny, and a tomboy, was always on the fringes of the girls. Maybe we all saw her as a possible future rival, or maybe just as someone we felt ill at ease with. When we started meeting together, she seemed so delighted, it had almost been embarrassing.

Olive got up to make coffee. "The two of you are so lucky," she said. "When I was growing up, there was no one to talk to, no one who could possibly understand where I was at. My brothers were ten and thirteen years older than me—more like uncles. I had sex when I was fourteen just as a way to get someone to talk to me. You don't know what that's like. You don't have that awful inner loneliness." Olive was so rarely self-pitying that we were both taken aback.

"But we're only children," Stuart pointed out.

"You have each other," she said. "You always have."

There was a silence. I don't know what Stuart was thinking. I was wondering in what way I "had" Stuart, when the kind of closeness we shared often made life ten times more painful than it might have been otherwise. If it hadn't been for that, I could have genuinely liked Ketti, different though we were. I wouldn't have had to feel my

40

stomach coil into knots when I saw her walk down the hall.

We finished dinner quietly, and then Stuart and I sat on the couch, shoulders touching, to watch a special on manatees while Olive went to her study to work.

TAVERN ON
THE GREEN

My father's last Saturday patient was at noon, and I met him to go to the park, looking for subjects for him to photograph.

My father had a mid-life hobby that was completely unexpected, but which, when you thought about it, was also directly connected to his personality. He had become an amateur street photographer. Using a zoom lens, he would find someone whose face he regarded as interesting and then zoom in extremely close, so that the entire photo showed only part of it—half a nose, an eye, a few strands of hair, the inside of an ear.

My father claimed that he knew the minute he saw someone if there was something about the face that intrigued him. He wasn't attracted to either freakishly peculiar people, as Diane Arbus was, or people who were unusually attractive. He never "did anything" with his photos, never entered them in shows or tried to turn his hobby into a part-time profession. It was just, he said, "a thing I like to do," and that was as far as he ever went toward explaining it. My mother, of course, thought his hobby bordered on insanity. I would find her looking with real concern at an eight-by-ten enlargement of an earlobe lying on my father's desk, saying, half to herself, "Sometimes I just wonder . . ."

My father said he liked having me along on these expeditions, and I enjoyed it too, noticing leaves and trees and aspects of nature I normally would have ignored. I started spotting possible subjects myself, although without my father I was such a daydreamer that I didn't see most human beings as I walked down the street. Sometimes, like today, he would be afraid the person was going to get up before he had had a chance to find the perfect angle for a photo. Then he would enlist me as an actual participant. "That old man," he murmured. "He's feeding the pigeons, but the bag is almost empty. Go over and sit beside him, and talk to him a bit. Tell him you like birds, whatever."

I went over to the old man and sat down. It seemed unfair of my father to make me take part, when I was so agonizingly ill at ease with strangers, but it was easier knowing it was for a purpose. "Do you give them cracker crumbs?" I asked. "I always heard they liked bread crumbs better."

The old man turned to look at me. I didn't know if this was what appealed to my father, but one of his eyes, perhaps due to a stroke, was practically glued shut, and the other was wide open and clear. He had funny spiky eyebrows that stood straight out, hanging over his eyes. "They don't care," he said. "Crackers, bread . . . just crumble it up fine. They can choke, you know, especially if they're hungry. Just give them a handful at a time."

"Do you . . . come here every day?" I asked. "I haven't seen you." He really reeked. Perhaps he was homeless. Another photographer might have seen him as a social commentary on poverty in Manhattan, or the eccentric little joys of old age. My father was probably just photographing his left eyebrow.

"Here, there." He grinned a gap-toothed smile. "Wherever." Then he looked up. "There's some funny man over there taking our photo," he said. "See him? See that little man in the bushes?"

I pretended to look. "Yes, well, I'm not sure who he's photographing."

The old man didn't seem bothered. "It's a funny thing with my eyes," he said. "Now that I'm old, I can see hundreds of yards away. Some kind of reverse thing with my vision. That man there, he has little Scotties on his tie, red ones and green ones. Wonder why people wear ties like that."

I couldn't believe it. That was exactly what my father did have on his tie. "I hate being photographed," I said suddenly.

"Do you?" He looked surprised. "Want me to go over and tell him to go away? He's probably after you. There are a lot of them like that. They go for the young girls, like to look at their pictures."

The thought of my father taking pictures with that aim was enough to make me smile. "No, I don't mind. . . . I don't think I'm the type, really."

The old man patted my knee. "Sure you are," he said, as though I had been asking for reassurance—maybe I had. "Make no mistake."

I was looking down at one of the pigeons pecking up some crumbs at our feet. I've always hated pigeons and squirrels—they seem mean and small-minded. It's hard for me to understand anyone feeling affection for them. "Do the same ones come every day?" I asked. "Or can't you tell?"

"Oh sure, I can tell," the old man said. "That one there, the one with the ruffled-out feathers, that's Mildred. . . . That one next to her, right behind her, is Morris. I don't think they're a couple, but they tend to come together. Maybe they're brother and sister." He chuckled. "I guess you think it's pretty dim-witted, making up names for these critters, but the way I look at it is it isn't doing any harm, and it's not like I'm giving them more brainpower than they have. They're pigeons, that's all. Birdbrains." He cackled.

"I used to have imaginary animals when I was little," I confided, "but I never had any real pets."

He looked concerned. "Not even a cat or a dog? What was the problem? Your parents wouldn't let you?"

"My mother's allergic to cats, and she was afraid I

44

wouldn't really walk a dog, and she would get stuck with it."

The old man flung out a handful of crumbs. "Yup, mothers are like that," he said.

I wasn't sure if he meant mothers had a tendency to allergies or a tendency to doubt how responsible their children would be. But I saw my father nod his head to one side, which was our agreed-upon gesture that he had taken all the photos he needed. I stood up. "I guess I should be getting home," I said. "Nice talking to you."

He doffed an imaginary hat. "My pleasure." He beckoned to me and added in a whisper, "Look out for the fellow in the bushes. He's got his eye on you. Stay clear of him, know what I mean?"

"Thanks, I will."

I took the path that led straight out of the park instead of meeting my father at the place where we had separated. He looked puzzled when he emerged. I explained how the old man had thought he had designs on me. "That's thoughtful," my father said. "I could have, I suppose. . . . I didn't think he'd see me so far away."

"He said his vision has gotten much better in old age."

"Yes, that happens to some people," my father said.

We walked into the park again, but this time my father kept me with him as he angled in on a woman in a big hat, a child playing in the grass, a man half hidden behind a newspaper. "Your mother thinks this is peculiar," he said. "She thinks I see parts and not the whole. Which is true. But I don't consider it a crime. Now that I'm almost fifty, I've decided why not indulge one's whims, as long as they aren't pathological."

"Why not?" I said.

"You're like me, and she's afraid you've picked it up from me. Using the zoom lens, for instance, keeping one's distance from people. But intimacy is a double-edged sword."

I sighed, thinking of Olive, wishing I were like her, getting involved without weighing the consequences, being easily physical without being afraid. "I wish I were different," I blurted out.

My father's expression softened. "Yes, well, you will be. It will all come in time. Nothing to worry about."

Our conversations were always like this, so indirect that if we hadn't had a long history of talking this way, it would have been unclear exactly what we were talking about. He was saying that he hoped one day I would marry for love and find joy in it, as he hadn't. "It's funny having Olive across the hall," I said. "It's like having two mothers."

"Too bad you didn't have two fathers," he said with a sad smile.

I squeezed his arm. "One is fine."

I couldn't imagine a male Olive, a hearty, back-slapping, gregarious father who would admire my clothes and be suspicious of my boyfriends.

As we were walking along Central Park West, we passed Gregory Arrington. My father didn't know who he was, and I would have been willing to pretend not to see him, but he saw us and stopped. "Hi, Isabel!" he said, in that slightly too loud, self-conscious voice he had. "I just read your poems in the *Whitman* folder. They were wonderful!" To my father, he said, "Your daughter's a terrific poet, Mr. Lear."

My father beamed. "I should say."

Gregory leaned forward and pumped my father's hand. "I'm Gregory Arrington. I write poetry too, so Isabel and I are kindred spirits, you could say."

I cringed inwardly, but my father, amazingly, said, "Yes, I remember your work from last year's yearbook. I liked the one about the couple melting into the rock." And to Gregory's and my stupefaction, he quoted several lines by heart.

I thought Gregory was going to fall at my father's feet. "God, thanks so much! I can't *believe* you really read it that carefully. My own parents hardly even— This has really made my day, or even, probably, my year."

"Of course," my father said in his typically dry way, "I'm an ophthalmologist, what do I know?"

"No," Gregory said. "You're wrong there. We write for people like you, the intelligent, sensitive person. It's awful just to be read and appreciated by other poets. That's what my aunt Yvonne says."

46

Gregory's aunt had won the Yale Younger Poets award several decades ago, and had had a kind of minor career since then; he worshiped her. "Listen," he said, perhaps carried away by my father's praise, "I'd love to take the two of you to lunch. Would you let me? I'd consider it an honor."

"Take Isabel," my father said expansively, offering me without seeming to have any doubt about my feelings. "I have a few little errands that, alas, must be attended to."

Whether he did or he didn't, I realized I could have invented some similar excuse, but Gregory looked so hopeful and pleased at my father's proffering of me that I smiled and said, "I'd love to."

After my father had disappeared, Gregory said, "How about Tavern on the Green?"

"Isn't that horribly expensive?" Despite having lived in New York all my life, I had never eaten there. My parents rarely ate out, and I'd always thought of it as a tourist place, though I liked the way they strung little lights in the trees in wintertime.

Gregory looked embarrassed. "It's my birthday," he said.

"Oh . . . Well, are you sure—"

"It's no big deal. I'm just seventeen. . . . How old are you?"

"I was seventeen last May."

"An older woman." He smiled. "This is, like, one of those amazing, serendipitous occasions, the kind you wrote about in that poem 'Hail.' I mean, October happens to be my favorite month, not just because I was born then. I love this kind of cool, overcast weather. And then your father remembering my poem." He sighed. He really seemed overcome.

I wondered if I had played a role in the serendipity of it all, if Gregory had a crush on me, as my friends would have liked, if behind the horrendous "kindred spirit" remark were some romantic yearnings. I didn't really know him well, and it wasn't fair of me to recoil from the idea of us as a couple. So we both wrote poetry? That didn't make us outcasts. But I remembered how Lois, who's five feet one, said she always felt suspicious when very short boys asked her out, because

47

she felt they might not have if she'd been a foot taller. Would Gregory have had whatever feelings he had for me if I had been dumb, or just average in intelligence? I knew that lots of intellectual boys preferred dumb girls, but I suspected Gregory was the opposite kind, who wanted someone who could understand what he was saying and feeling. Let me fall in love with him, I asked some imaginary deity. Let me find him sexy.

We had a lavish lunch. Gregory's parents were rich, and I was hungry. We had oysters and a warm lobster salad, with fresh pineapple sherbet for dessert. Gregory was less awkward about this kind of situation than he was in much more ordinary ones at school. What was awkward about him was partly his appearance. He was so extremely tall—six feet five—that he clearly felt some degree of alienation from his body. His head was small, and he had weirdly long fingers, almost like some monster in a sci-fi movie. And there was something unsettling in his stare. He didn't seem able not to be intense, even when we were discussing something totally mundane. By the end of the lunch I knew he had a crush on me as definitely as if he had told me—though, of course, he hadn't.

"I was really impressed by your father," he said. "He seems like a man with so many facets." (I'd told him about the photographic expeditions.) "I don't think my father's ever read a poem *I've* written, or that *anyone* has written. Of course, he's a corporation lawyer, so what can you expect?"

"What does your mother do?" I asked. I was always more interested in that than in what fathers did.

He hesitated, as though it were a complicated question. "She takes courses," he said. He gulped some sparkling water, and I watched his Adam's apple bob up and down. "My father is your standard type—zigzagging around, using people. He has girlfriends, mistresses, whatever you call them. . . . And my mother is just this very sensitive, self-doubting person who can't see that he's full of shit, that he isn't worthy of being in the same *room* with her. She's in awe of him! It's so disgusting, it's so *sad* . . ."

Gregory spoke in great bursts of feeling that seemed to jet

out of him. "Does she, uh, know about his girlfriends?" I asked, thinking how ordinary my own parents seemed, even in their eccentricities and their not especially happy marriage.

"Naturally!" He sighed. "He flaunts it—he's some kind of sadist. And of course he has contempt for me, he thinks I'm worthless. This is a terrible thing to say, but if I could do it without going to jail, without anyone knowing, I'd kill my father." He looked at me. "Is that the worst thing you've ever heard anyone say? Do you hate me? I do have monstrous thoughts about some things. . . . But I get the idea you have strong feelings too, Isabel, even though you're pretty quiet—not about killing people, but just—"

"He sounds like a terrible person," I said, not quite answering what he was asking.

"He has contempt for me because I'm a virgin," Gregory said. "Can you believe this? He offered to take me to a call girl when I turned sixteen. The idea of worshiping a woman, respecting her, loving her mind as well as her body—that's beyond his ken. He's an animal." His voice had risen, quivering with intensity, and I saw a nearby couple, who looked yuppyish and self-satisfied, smile. "Of course, we're all animals," he added in a much lower voice. "I wasn't implying that I thought—"

"No, I know," I said. I did. I knew, or understood, everything he was saying, but it was too painfully close. He was everything about myself that I hated, or questioned, or wanted to disappear. But even as I was thinking that, I was wondering if I should go to bed with him, to do both of us a favor. It wasn't the thought of sacrificing my virginity to someone I didn't love that held me back as much as the fear that for the rest of the year Gregory would stare at me with such palpable yearning that everyone in school would know.

We sat in silence. "This is one of the happiest days of my life," Gregory said. "I know those things should be left unsaid . . . but why *not* say them occasionally? Why save emotions just for poetry?"

"Right." I smiled at him, feeling not just six months but, in some ways, six years older.

We walked back through the park. At one point Gregory reached out and furtively grabbed my hand, and I let that happen. His hand was so large, my own felt imprisoned, but it was more than just gratitude for the lunch that kept me from pulling away. I felt fond of him.

I felt awkward only when, as we approached our building, I saw Olive's Jerry coming down the street. I disentangled myself and thanked Gregory for the lunch. He beamed and said he would call me.

Jerry and I shared the elevator going up to "our" floor. "I thought Stuart was your boyfriend," he said.

"No, we're just friends . . . and so is the person you saw me with. We had lunch together because it happens to be his birthday."

"Where'd you go?"

"Tavern on the Green—his parents are rich," I added stupidly.

Jerry grinned. "Can't hurt. I always tried to fall in love with rich girls, but it never took."

"We're not in love," I said earnestly. "We're not even—"

Jerry squeezed my shoulder. "Hey, baby, calm down. I won't tell. He's smitten with you. You're maybe not so smitten with him . . . yet. Maybe you will be in time. Maybe not. Don't get excited."

"I'm not!" But I was. Suddenly I felt confused and shaky. I hated the thought of Jerry telling Olive, and Olive telling Stuart, and Stuart teasing me about it. I wanted a private life that no one would know about, some secret lover so amazingly unlike anyone my friends would think of for me that if they knew, they would be agog: a sixty-year-old businessman, a waiter, a hairdresser with a huge, gleaming smile.

My mother was home from her job, going through her mail. "Now where is your father?" she said, as though he were a dog I had gone out to walk and had returned without.

I shrugged. "I was with him early this afternoon, then I had lunch with a friend. He said he was going to do some errands."

She sighed. "God only knows what *that* means." She looked at her watch. "It's four and we have a dinner date.

And naturally he won't wear a watch. He says he doesn't want to feel imprisoned by the laws of time. Can you tell me how not wearing a watch frees one from time?''

The idea that I could be an impartial, Solomon-like judge of what was peculiar about either of my parents was strange to me. I knew my father didn't wear a watch, I knew his theory about being free without one, I knew it exasperated my mother. "I think he'll be home soon," I said with well-practiced diplomacy. "I think he said about five o'clock."

I wanted to lie down. I wanted to encourage visions of Gregory in a loverlike posture to dance around in my head. "I'm going to take a nap," I said.

THE BEGINNING OF
SOMETHING

I wasn't sure whether to tell anyone except Lois about my lunch with Gregory. I was still torn between describing it as the possible beginning of something and calling it just an isolated event of the weekend. But by the end of Monday more or less everyone knew. It started in Contemporary History, when Mr. Battin made some remark about the ill-timed and misconceived efforts of the antiwar activists during the Vietnam War, how their actions had only "confused" matters and helped prolong rather than shorten the war.

My parents had been active in the anti–Vietnam War movement. You couldn't have found a couple less like the ones Mr. Battin was describing, who were supposedly all drug-crazed flower children who gave peculiar astrological names to their children and allowed them to run about naked. My hand shot up, seemingly of its own volition, and I counterattacked. As a student I'm more the type who hands in excellent papers and doesn't speak in class unless called upon. I could hear my voice shaking from emotion as I made my point.

"You seen to be quite an expert on this, Isabel," Mr.

Battin said. He was a small man with a throaty voice. Contemporary History was as "ancient" to him as events of medieval Prussia. It was said he had, years ago, completed all the course requirements for a doctorate but never finished his dissertation. Hence his having to teach at Whitman when he clearly loathed teenagers. "Could you give us your sources?"

I started to when unexpectedly Gregory, who was one of Mr. Battin's favorites, raised his hand. "You're always telling us to question the media, Mr. Battin," he said, "but what you're saying sounds just like what President Johnson wanted the American public to believe. And you're also always saying if we don't learn from history, we're condemned to repeat it. Isn't that just what we're in danger of doing now with the Contras? If it hadn't been for Isabel's parents, and other brave, idealistic people, maybe Reagan would have felt able to go even further, and get us involved in another Vietnam."

Mr. Battin thought Reagan was a fool. It was hard to find a president he admired other than Thomas Jefferson, and even about him he had some doubts. "Isn't that a little extreme, Gregory?" he said. "I feel—"

Just then the bell rang. Mr. Battin looked relieved, as he usually did when the class was over. I passed Gregory on the way out and smiled weakly. "Thanks."

His Adam's apple bobbed up and down. "I'm so glad you made that statement," he said. "No one *ever* challenges him! He's so self-enclosed, with all his prejudices."

"He scares me," I admitted.

"He shouldn't," Gregory said heatedly. "You were wonderful."

I don't know if his voice rose on that last sentence, or if everyone had picked up on his coming to my defense, but by lunchtime—Gregory had second lunch, I had first—Andria, Ketti, and Lois surrounded me. "God, I couldn't believe it," Andria said. "Did you seduce him, or what? Taking on Battin! He's going to be putting cloaks in mud puddles for you next, Iz."

I was picking over my macaroni and cheese. "We had lunch together," I said. I described our encounter.

"I was sitting behind him in English," Ketti said, "and he spent the whole period staring at you, drawing your picture. Talk about gone!"

Only Lois looked at me in her usual thoughtful, hesitant way, and asked, "But is it mutual?"

I shrugged. "Well, certainly not totally. I just—"

"Give him a chance," Andria said. "He deserves it. . . . And he's smart. He's practically the only guy in the school who's your intellectual equal."

I had a horrible image of the two "brains" marching off together to discuss sestinas or isosceles triangles in bed. "I want a hunk," I said wryly. "Gregory's too much like me. He's so—"

"You do *not* want a hunk," Lois said. "You *know* you don't."

Ketti never bought lunch. She brought her own soy-milk shake and raw, healthy veggies in a Ziploc bag. "Stuart thinks Gregory isn't right for you," she said. "He thinks you need someone more suave and playful."

"When did he say that?" Lois asked, picking up on it.

"After history class." She plucked a radish out of her bag.

I hated learning that Stuart's first impulse had been to discuss the incident with Ketti. "Stuart doesn't even *know* Gregory," I snapped.

"That's what I told him," Ketti said. "Anyway, who's suave and playful outside of Cary Grant movies? No one at Whitman, for sure."

Andria was eating a huge helping of macaroni and cheese. She genuinely liked school food. "I bet Gregory has hidden depths," she said.

Ketti giggled. "He better."

"What does that mean?" Lois said indignantly. "I think Gregory's really interesting looking. He's just awkward."

What was sweet about that remark was that in sixth grade, Lois and I had drawn up a list of the future destinies of everyone in our class. For ourselves we had predicted interesting, intense men with offbeat senses of humor. About

54

Gregory we had written, "He looks like Abraham Lincoln, the week after he was shot."

"I'll play it by ear," I said.

"Don't just toss him aside," Andria said. "You all think Hal and I knew we were meant for each other, but it isn't like that. For a long time I mainly felt sorry for him. I was touched that anyone could like me that much."

We all stared at her in surprise.

"It was all just superficial things," Andria went on calmly. "Like he has moles on his back, or that he hates plays. And he's always treating his older brother as this expert on everything, whereas he's really a conceited jerk. But who cares about any of that? When you're in love, those things don't seem to matter anymore."

We were silent. None of us had the authority to question Andria. Ketti had had more sexual experience, but according to her she'd never been "really in love." I wondered about everything Andria had said. Those didn't sound like little things to me at all; they sounded large, insupportable. How could I ever love anyone who didn't like plays? And could one really ignore moles? Not that they would be crucial, but I couldn't see how one would cease to notice them. What I feared more than anything was not failure to be chosen, or even being chosen by the wrong person, but my own tendency to criticize everyone inwardly. I know that's a classic defense of shy people, but I was afraid that by now it was embedded in me, that same little voice that for years had criticized my parents' marriage and wondered why they had stayed together.

"I don't think I'll ever love anyone the way you love Hal," Ketti said dispassionately. "I do notice those petty things. I'm never swept away."

I was relieved at her saying that, even though in my mind she was becoming "the rival."

"Oh come on," Lois said. "Those are clichés. I don't even think that's what Andria meant. She meant you notice them, but you don't care."

Andria was munching on a green apple. "Nope, that's not what I meant," she said. "I guess I'm just not that critical a person. I think once you decide that this person is it, the one, whatever, you don't keep picking him apart in your mind any more than you keep picking at yourself for not being able to stop biting your nails." Andria's bitten nails were the only physical sign that all was not totally smooth sailing within. Without them, we might have hated her.

"But I do it to myself," Lois said. "I criticize myself all the time."

"Just give Gregory a chance," Andria said, ignoring this remark, "that's all I'm asking."

"I will," I promised.

I saw Ketti watching me. "But, like, physically, does he . . . I mean, if there's not that—"

"I don't agree," Lois said. "I think if you love someone, all that might not be so important."

I mainly wished that all this were not so public, that it had not been Gregory who had been "selected" for me by my friends, as in some kind of eighteenth-century arranged marriage. I wished he were, if not suave, at least more able to conceal his feelings. Intensity seemed to come shooting out of him, even when he didn't speak. In the afternoon I became conscious of his eyes boring into me from behind. If I said anything in class, he backed me up, even if there was no need to. I felt I knew what he had been feeling: that he was destined to be the awkward outcast, at least until college, maybe until he was in his twenties and published, when I, just by strolling down Central Park West with a father who had happened to memorize some lines from one of his poems, had appeared to beckon him out of the darkness.

After school I managed to avoid everyone, Gregory as well as the foursome, by claiming I had to meet my mother at her job. I lied more than people realized, but evidently I had what appeared to my friends an honest character, and they didn't question me. And then, perhaps to turn the lie into a truth, I decided to stop by the Institute since my mother finished at four on Mondays. When she saw me, she looked startled. "Is anything wrong?"

I felt guilty at that, but it was true. I almost never went on expeditions with my mother the way I did with my father. The one activity mothers and daughters often share—shopping for clothes—was something I loved to do with Olive but never did with my mother.

"I'm fine," I said. "I thought we might walk home, if you're ready to leave."

She smiled. "I'd like that." The Institute was on the East Side, and it was a pleasant twenty-minute stroll home through Central Park.

My mother walked briskly, and she often called my attention to a particular tree or bunch of flowers. I think this was because she had grown up in the country and felt, as she said, "imprisoned" in the city. She wasn't afraid of muggers. She claimed that if you walked rapidly and looked self-confident, no one would attack you.

"Have you met with Ms. Evarts yet?" she asked. Ms. Evarts was our college counselor.

I shook my head. "I pretty much know where I want to apply," I said. "I've made appointments for the interviews."

"But she might know of some places you haven't thought of," my mother said. "Your father has this bee in his bonnet about the Ivy League, but you ought to know, Isabel, that almost none of our friends went to those schools. It's all so petty and snobbish. Who cares?"

I wondered if this was an indirect reference to the fact that my father was Jewish, and Princeton had had a reputation for being anti-Semitic. He claimed he had never noticed it, but my mother would have said my father just didn't notice things. "I agree," I said. "I mean, I'm keeping an open mind."

"It's who you are," she insisted, as though I had disagreed rather than agreed, "what you make of yourself, not all those labels people stick on you. Then, if you make it, you know you've done it on your own. You can be proud of that." Her cheeks were pink from the chilly air.

I wondered if she meant that she was proud of herself; she never talked about that. "Do you ever . . . regret that you didn't, you know, do something earlier, I mean before I was born, or right after, so that now . . ." I was inarticulate

57

talking to my mother about personal things. I wasn't sure I wanted to know.

"Well, but I had you," she said, puzzled.

"No, I just meant . . . nowadays some women go straight on. They only take a few weeks off from work and get someone to care for the baby. You could have afforded that, couldn't you?"

"But think of those children!" my mother exclaimed. "No one home when they return from school, or some indifferent woman plunking them in front of the TV, letting them gorge on snacks to pacify them. . . . Like Stuart."

I laughed nervously. "What do you mean? He isn't so fat."

"Yes, but he's never for one *day* of his life known what a normal family life is like. Now I'm not blaming Olive, totally. She *had* to work. She married an irresponsible man. But still—why do you think he's over at our house so often? We've given him a sense of roots, of something solid that will be there forever."

I could have said that I probably had had as many meals at Olive's and for the same reason—wanting a contrast. I wanted to be allowed to eat rich, unbalanced meals with wine and candlelight, to have a sense that a family didn't have to be the grim triangle that it seemed to be with me and my parents. "I suppose everyone needs both," I said vaguely.

"Both what?" my mother demanded.

I looked into her gray-blue eyes. I felt as I had with Mr. Battin, frightened, tongue-tied, wanting, somehow, to defy my mother, to insist on her knowing how much I loved Olive, how dreary my childhood would have been without her. "That there can be different lifestyles," I stammered.

We were nearing our apartment. "You know one of the most touching things Olive ever said to me?" my mother said. "She said, 'You have two things that I always wanted, and I'll never have: a lifelong relationship with one person, and a daughter.' " My mother smiled.

"Didn't you always want a son?" I couldn't resist asking.

"Not in the same way," she replied. "Because sons leave. . . . Which is why it's been nice for me, having Stuart

58

so nearby. Not having all the worries about him the way I would if he were my own, but being able to enjoy his company. When you took ballet lessons, he used to come over and sit and play with his toy trucks while I did the ironing. He'd just come over and sit there, on the floor, talking to himself . . ." She trailed off dreamily.

"What would you worry about if he were your actual son?" I asked.

"Oh, everything!" my mother exclaimed. "Drunken driving. What if he killed someone? Drugs. . . . Getting involved with the wrong kind of girl, even getting her pregnant. That still happens, you know."

"Don't you worry about any of that with me?" I asked wryly. I'd always thought parents worried more about daughters.

My mother just smiled indulgently. "What would I worry about with you?" she asked.

Naturally it wasn't meant to be an insult. She just meant that I had not had a history of sneaking in at three in the morning, or smoking pot in the bathroom, or emerging from my bedroom with guys in black leather jackets. Still, I felt crushed. It seemed part of my lonesomely predictable image that I kept trying, at least mentally, to shake off.

CATCH AS CATCH CAN

By Thanksgiving Gregory and I were considered a couple. We went out on dates, we kissed, we talked about our hopes and ambitions. I was to win the National Book Award at twenty-five; he was to get a Guggenheim and live in Rome. It was nice to have someone to share these grandiose and peculiar fantasies with. Marriage, children, love—all that would happen, or it wouldn't, and, we agreed, it didn't matter all that much.

My mother had invited Olive, Jerry, and Stuart for Thanksgiving dinner, but they were going to Jerry's mother's. She lived in a large house in Amagansett with her second husband. "Well, it must be serious, then," my mother said.

"What must be?" my father asked, continuing to read, his mind obviously "on hold," as it often seemed to be in conversations with my mother.

"If they're going to Jerry's mother's for Thanksgiving, maybe it's serious."

"Who's Jerry?" my father asked.

"Sid, really. . . . She's been seeing him for over three

60

months. Olive! Do you remember who Olive is?'' she asked sarcastically.

"Oh, Jerry, the aging hippie,'' my father said. "Serious? Never.''

My mother looked exasperated, although she had called Jerry the very same thing several months earlier. "Are you going by his beard? By his gold chain?'' she said. "Those are just outward appurtenances.''

I was surprised, because my mother, more than my father, judged people by how they dressed and comported themselves. "They seem to be happy,'' my father said, retreating.

"Do *you* think it's serious?'' my mother asked me. I was sitting in an armchair, doing my history assignment.

"In the sense of leading to marriage? I don't know. I haven't asked. . . . He *is* around a lot.'' Privately I agreed with my father. I saw Jerry's tenure in Olive's life as time-limited, but I thought she seemed happy, and I didn't mind him as much as I had in the beginning. Deep down I was still rooting for Chester to make a comeback.

We had a nice Thanksgiving. I was freed after dinner and went to a movie with Lois and her father, which diluted the familyness of the day and made it bearable. The following day, Friday, my mother wondered if Stuart might want to come over for a "catch-as-catch-can'' dinner.

"Go see if he's there,'' she suggested. "It's turkey curry with that pear chutney Stuart likes. And I'm making the lemon pie he's so fond of, the one *without* the meringue.''

It was midafternoon, and I'd been getting that sleepy feeling that comes from being indoors all day. Outside it looked bleak and cold. I knew I'd feel better if I took a brisk walk, but I couldn't bear the effort of getting dressed in sweaters and boots and scarves and gloves. Instead I strolled across the hallway and knocked on Stuart's door. There was no answer, no sound of voices within, or the radio, or anyone moving around. Probably, I decided, they were spending the entire weekend at Jerry's mother's. I felt disappointed. I'd been looking forward to seeing Stuart. On the off chance, I knocked again, harder.

61

This time Stuart came to the door. He looked sleepy-eyed and was barefoot, wearing jeans and a shirt that was hanging out on one side and buttoned wrong. When he saw me, a peculiar, almost frightened expression passed over his face. "Hi," he said nervously.

"My mother wondered if you could come for dinner tonight," I said, puzzled. "We weren't sure if you were back."

He looked around. "Oh yeah, I'm back. . . . Olive and Jerry decided to stay till tomorrow. What, um, what time? Did you say dinner?"

"I did. . . . Seven?"

Stuart seemed to be trying to summon his usual joking self-composure but without much success. I wished very much he would. "Terrific," he said heartily. "Seven's perfect." For one second we just stood there, staring at each other. His eyes told me he had been in bed with someone, and that someone was undoubtedly Ketti. "See you then."

I returned to our apartment sick with rage and jealousy. "He can come," I told my mother grimly. She was in the kitchen making the crust for the pie.

"Oh, wonderful!" she said. "Isabel, you always said you wanted to learn to make crust for a pie. Why don't you watch me? It's really not complicated."

"I never said I wanted to learn to make crust," I yelled. "Why should I want to learn that?"

My mother frowned. "Because someday . . . Well, most men love pie, and someday—"

"Someday *what*?" I stared at her fiercely.

"You might be married," she said.

"Someday I will *not* be married," I said, "and I'm only marrying a man who makes his own crust." With that, I stormed out of the room. Shortly afterward I said I was going for a walk.

"Bundle up!" my father called cheerfully. He had the capacity to sit for hours in the same chair, not even changing his position. "One day you will grow into that chair," my mother warned him. "You will become one thing, one unit."

In a weird way I envied both of them: my father for his

62

ability to love a day like today when nothing was happening; my mother for taking such idiotic pride in her domestic skills, for probably thinking, as she rolled out her crust, how unusual it was for a modern woman both to have a respected job and to make pies from scratch. I stomped along Central Park West, wishing that Stuart weren't too young to die of a heart attack while making love to someone, or that Ketti might have some really unpleasant, painful, communicable venereal disease—not lethal, but hideous nonetheless. I wished impotence on him, and on her more than semifrigidity. And as I wished these nasty things, the wind bit into my cheeks, my toes were freezing, and I was sure the two of them were rolling around in total ecstasy in Olive's huge snug bed with the puffy flowered comforter.

Suddenly I hated Olive for being as my mother had always said she was—footloose, not caring what her only son was up to in her absence, not even caring if he used her bed. What kind of mother *was* that? You suggested it, I reminded myself. I remembered my remark to Ketti, "Who are you aiming for? Stuart?" But I had said it because I thought it was so unlikely, because Ketti had always gone for broad-shouldered guys with squinty eyes who planned to go into the army, or join rock bands, instead of going to college, who lifted weights, or went out for track, or knew the right clubs to go to for dancing on weekends. If you hadn't made that stupid remark, I told myself, she never would have thought of him. And stupid Stuart, just giving in to whoever pursued him. How passive could you get? What fools men were! Even Stuart agreed with that; he ought to know.

I walked myself into a state of cold, miserable exhaustion, which was pleasing because it corresponded to my inner state. When I returned home, red-nosed, coughing, my father suggested I take a hot shower, and my mother wondered if I mightn't be getting my period. "I'm fine," I said contritely. "I'll just rest before dinner."

I was exhausted more than tired, and burrowing under the covers in the overheated bedroom after a shower was so soothing that I was asleep in a second. I woke up to find Stuart kneeling beside the bed. He bent over and gave me an Eskimo kiss. "Curry time," he said gently.

I sat bolt upright. "What are you doing here?" I demanded.

He looked surprised. "I was invited for dinner—remember? It's a quarter past seven."

But he no longer looked guilty or flustered. He was wearing sneakers and socks, his shirt was neatly tucked in. "I hate Thanksgiving weekend," I said fiercely, running a brush over my hair.

Stuart grinned. "It's not that bad."

I wouldn't answer. I walked into the dining room, where my mother had set the table only slightly less elegantly than for Thanksgiving. She had put everything out on the buffet on hot plates. "Just help yourselves," she said gaily. "It's all piping hot."

Stuart heaped his plate with everything. "This is fantastic, Rosalie. I love curry."

My mother beamed. "I know you do." To me and my father she said, "Stuart helped me make this pear chutney. He mixed the pears and the raisins for me."

My father doffed an imaginary hat. "Superb. . . . So, how has *your* Thanksgiving been going, Stuart? You were away, I hear?"

Stuart was in the middle of chewing. "At Mom's boyfriend's mother's house. It's quite a place. A mansion, almost. Her first husband left her a lot of dough."

My father was eating precisely and slowly, as always. Sometimes my mother brought in dessert while he was still in the middle of his main course. He had a habit of lifting a fork with food on it to his lips and then, forgetfully, setting it down on his plate again. "And is there a replacement?" he asked.

"Yeah, she married again, this funny little guy who doesn't speak much. But he's nice to her. He's a professional bridge player."

"Then it must be serious," my mother said, reaching for a roll.

"Well, he makes his living at it," Stuart said.

My mother hesitated. "No, I meant between Olive and Jerry, her meeting his mother, I wondered—"

"Are they getting hitched is what she means," I interrupted hastily. "Is he going to make an honest woman of her?"

Stuart shrugged. "*Que será será.* I don't see him as permanent myself, but who am I to say?"

"Well, but you know her better than we do, better than anyone," my mother said. "You can tell if you think he's the right person for her."

"No," Stuart said. "I can't really."

My mother seemed stymied by this. She liked things neatly tied up. There was a pause. My father was eating with his eyes fixed on some inner space. "You've been through a lot," my mother said to Stuart, patting his hand. "You're a brave, good boy."

Stuart flashed a look at me that normally would have meant: We'll laugh at this in private. I pretended not to notice. I concentrated on eating my curry, made a few monosyllabic remarks, and put away a piece of lemon pie.

"God," Stuart said after a second helping. "This is the world's best lemon pie, Rosalie. Really. I've probably said that before, but it's true."

"You don't miss the meringue?" my mother asked, as she always did.

"Not at all. . . . That's what's wrong with most lemon pie, all that sticky white glop on top. And the crust is fantastic."

My mother smiled slyly at me. "I was going to teach Isabel how to make crust," she said, "but she felt like taking a walk."

Stuart shuddered. "In this weather? This was a day to stay in bed."

I glared at him.

After dinner I started to go back to my room. I heard Stuart murmur something to my mother and heard her murmur back, "I think she's getting her period." That seemed the last straw. First of all, I wasn't. Secondly, when I did, I never had cramps or moods, and third, how could my mother say something so totally personal to Stuart?

He followed me into my room. "Want to come over and watch *The Importance of Being Earnest*?" he said. "It's on at nine."

"It's on here too," I said.

"I thought you might be getting a little stir crazy. . . . I always do on vacations. Or I would if Olive and Jerry were around all the time. Not that your parents aren't swell, but—"

"Swell!" I whirled around. "What kind of word is that? They are not swell! They're crazy, and you know that as well as I do."

Stuart came over and stood so close to me I could feel his breath on my neck. "Just come over," he whispered. "We don't have to talk. I know you're mad at me."

I didn't say anything.

"Nothing is what it seems," he added enigmatically.

I was torn between denying everything and leaping at his throat. "I guess you had a pleasant afternoon," I said, choosing what seemed like a middle ground.

"Sure," he said. "It was good." He stood there awkwardly. "I thought . . . I would have thought Gregory would be coming over."

"He's in Seattle with his grandparents," I said.

"That must have been lonely, then," he said in that same caring, soothing voice. "I'm sorry."

I was really pleased at his handing me, free of charge, a way out. "Yeah, well, we aren't exactly—"

"Would he mind if you came over?" Stuart said. "Is that it?"

"No, no, not at all. What would there be to mind?" Suddenly I felt better. There was no real parallel between me and Gregory and Stuart and Ketti, but I was determined to pretend there was. I was even suddenly determined to make it happen.

My parents looked relieved and pleased when I emerged with Stuart and said we were going to watch *The Importance*

66

of Being Earnest. "Oh, maybe we will too," my mother said. "What a good idea. . . . Though I hate thinking of Wendy Hiller being old enough to play Lady Bracknell. Remember her in *Major Barbara*, Sid?"

"How could I forget?" my father said. "But Rex Harrison never deserved her. Neither did Leslie Howard in *Pygmalion*."

"Men never deserve women," my mother said.

Stuart laughed.

When we were in his apartment, he said spontaneously, "I love your family. I just can't help it. They're so—well, predictable, but also eccentric. They just go right on with all their little things."

"That's so condescending!" I said. "They have a rotten marriage, they never listen to each other. What's charming? What's delightful? That my father spends his spare time photographing earlobes, and my mother pretends you're her son? It's all sick!"

"Does she really pretend I'm her son?" Stuart asked, kicking off his sneakers and settling down on the couch. "Well, Olive thinks of you as her daughter—where's the harm?"

His face looked so rosy and self-satisfied that I felt like strangling him. I knew I could have played the role I often had—the good platonic friend, who would be eager to hear how it had gone with Ketti, if it had lived up to expectations, if this had been the first time. But I wasn't up to hearing nitty-gritty details, even if he was up to giving them. "Aren't things with Gregory going well?" Stuart asked tentatively, as though still wary of my mood. "He's clearly in love with you. He moons at you all during classes."

"Right, well, I like him too," I said. "He has a lot of depth. . . . And I think he's attractive."

"Is he, uh, pressuring you to, you know, go further than you feel like going?" Stuart asked. "Is that it?"

"Of course not," I said. "We're not at that stage at all." Then, remembering my earlier vow, I added, "Yet."

"Don't rush into things," Stuart advised. "Wait till you're really ready."

"Who's rushing?"

He was looking away. "You need someone special. Maybe Gregory's not the guy."

"Someone suave and playful?" I asked, raising my eyebrows.

He flushed. "I didn't mean—"

I sat up, my arms wrapped around my legs. "I don't like your discussing me with Ketti. Please don't."

"I'm sorry," he said. "I won't. . . . I was just—"

"Just *don't*," I insisted.

"Okay." The tension in the air seemed almost to quiver like a palpable force. "Ketti and I don't discuss and analyze things the way you and I do," he said finally.

"You just fuck," I said contemptuously.

"I didn't mean that. I meant you aren't being displaced as my . . ." He smiled weakly. "You aren't being displaced."

"I'm hugely relieved."

He was speaking more haltingly than usual, trying to explain what couldn't be explained. "Once you do it with Gregory, or whoever, you'll see . . . it doesn't necessarily mean total closeness in every way. It just means that certain things work, certain connections."

"It sounds like electrical wiring."

Relieved at my taking a lighter tone, Stuart grinned. "Right—sparks, fuses blowing."

Smiling, I said, "Maybe I *will* do it with Gregory. I'm just afraid he'll be even worse then."

"Blind adoration *can* be a major pain," Stuart agreed. "What I like about Ketti—"

"But I *like* that about Gregory!" I exclaimed, coming unexpectedly to his defense. "I *like* that he has feelings, and he's not afraid to show them. It's not all just games and fooling around with him."

"Yeah, if that's all it is with you, you'll break his heart," Stuart said. "That wouldn't be kind, would it?"

"Maybe I'll fall madly in love with him, maybe I'll become sex crazed and demented."

Stuart smiled. "Give it a try, Iz. Go for it."

It seemed pointless to make an all-out effort to seduce

Gregory just to get Stuart jealous with no guarantee I would succeed. I would only do it, I promised myself, if *I* wanted to. But I had to admit the idea of breaking someone's heart was sort of appealing.

PRINCETON

Gregory and I were going to visit Princeton the following weekend. When I told Mr. O'Reilly, he said, "Tell you what—unless this would wreck the whole thing for you. I have a friend who lives there, the director of the art museum. I'll drive you down, unless you want to take the train, and he can put us all up at his house."

I felt embarrassed. "I think we'll stay in the dorms, just to talk to the kids, but we'd love to drive down with you."

I wasn't sure Gregory would love it, but I preferred it to the idea of a two-hour train ride each way. Gregory said it would be fine. He admired Mr. O'Reilly tremendously. "Do you really think he's gay?" he said. "How can you tell?"

"How can you tell anything?" I said. I was becoming more critical of Gregory now that I had decided, unbeknownst to him, to sleep with him.

"He never talks about it," Gregory said. "Even obliquely. . . . But you could be right."

I had never had an ardent admirer before. Maybe I wasn't the type for it. I still couldn't get used to Gregory's meaningful stares as we passed in the halls, or the way he tried to find something in whatever I said to agree with, even when I was being contradictory or perverse. I wanted him to put up a struggle. "Would you rather take the train?" I asked.

"I want to do whatever you want to do," Gregory said.

"But you must have some feeling about it," I said, exasperated. "Tell me what you want!"

He looked anguished, wanting desperately to please me but not sure how. "Let's drive," he said. "That sounds like fun." And he squeezed my hand in his huge paw.

Mr. O'Reilly's car was a red BMW, jazzier than I would have expected, and he turned out to be a speed demon. It was as if I were to discover that Gregory wore skintight purple Calvin Klein briefs. We sat in the back and Gregory, sensing my nervousness, put his arm around me and held my hand. "Am I going too fast for you?" Mr. O'Reilly called out, glancing at us with a slight smile in the rearview mirror.

"We're fine," Gregory said. His hands were icy cold, but I didn't know if that was because of being with me or because of Mr. O'Reilly's driving.

Gregory wanted us to stay with Mr. O'Reilly's friend. I think he felt that would be more private, whereas it seemed to me the other way around. "Is this friend of yours someone you knew from college?" Like my father, Mr. O'Reilly had gone to Princeton.

"From prep school," Mr. O'Reilly said. "Deerfield."

"My father went there," Gregory said. He snorted derisively, as he usually did when he mentioned his father. "He flunked out."

"Yes, there were a lot of those," Mr. O'Reilly said. "Spoiled, rich, corrupt boys . . . I went back for the twenty-fifth reunion and they're all merchants of commerce now, staggeringly successful, and somewhere to the right of Attila the Hun in their politics. It's sad how predictable life is sometimes."

Gregory and I had talked about wanting to come back to our twenty-fifth Whitman reunion successful and self-possessed, published poets. Everyone would have read our books and would gather around, asking for our autographs. "I thought it was supposed to be the opposite," I said. "I thought prom queens went to seed, and football stars took to drink and gained two hundred pounds.''

"And sensitive, awkward outcasts blossomed like birds of paradise?'' Mr. O'Reilly sneered. "Perhaps occasionally.''

I wondered why he was being so mean. I knew he liked the two of us better than anyone else in the school. Why should he begrudge us, even in fantasy, a triumphal reentry into Whitman? "You must have been miserable at Deerfield,'' I said, to get back at him.

"I wasn't miserable exactly,'' Mr. O'Reilly said. "But then, I wasn't a track star, or president of my class, either. I got along, I was innocuous. When I went back for the reunion, no one remembered who I was. If Pablo hadn't dragged me, I never would have gone.''

Pablo was his friend in Princeton, the one Mr. O'Reilly was staying with. Pablo's parents, Mr. O'Reilly told us, had been left-wingers, his father fought in the republican army in the Spanish Civil War. "I guess being foreign must have been tough too,'' Gregory said.

"You mean for me?'' Mr. O'Reilly said. "Being from Arkansas?''

"No, I meant your friend . . . wasn't he brought up in Spain?''

"Oh, but that gave him a certain panache. Better Spain than Arkansas, I can assure you. . . . Where do *your* parents stand in the political sphere, Gregory? Are they pinkos like Isabel's?''

The fact was that Mr. O'Reilly was liberal—he even belonged to the same nuclear freeze group my father did—but he somehow enjoyed mocking that, like everything else. "God no,'' Gregory said. "Well, my mother sneaks out, occasionally, and votes Democratic, and it's supposedly this big family secret, but my dad's more of the Attila the Hun school.''

"Of course,'' Mr. O'Reilly said. "I should have guessed.'' He zipped ahead of two cars that were going sixty miles an hour in order to get to the outside lane.

"My father isn't stupid,'' Gregory said, "he's just . . .

72

crude. I mean, he doesn't use his mind to contemplate things. He—''

Zipping back to the other lane, Mr. O'Reilly said imperturbably, ''What is perhaps striking about men like your father is they are not burdened by self-loathing.''

''But he *ought* to be burdened by self-loathing,'' Gregory said, sitting forward. ''He's loathsome!''

''No,'' Mr. O'Reilly said abruptly, ''that never helps.'' He reached over and put in a tape of Elizabeth Schwarzkopf singing arias from *Così fan tutte* and concentrated on the driving and the music for the rest of the way.

Pablo Rodríguez was fat, with big dancing black eyes, and almost bald, like a village priest in a Spanish film, but more urbane. He hugged Mr. O'Reilly and then hugged both of us. I was amazed Mr. O'Reilly could have such an exuberant, outgoing friend. ''Welcome, little ones!'' he said, somewhat ironically, since he was about a foot shorter than Gregory. ''Come in, come in.''

Mr. O'Reilly explained that we wanted to stay at the dorm.

Pablo looked hurt. ''Why? The dorm? I have four guest bedrooms, perfect privacy, I'm an excellent cook.''

''We thought we might talk to some of the students,'' Gregory said, looking torn.

''By all means, talk to them,'' Pablo said, carrying in my bag. ''But afterward, you must return here for a good night's sleep. The door is open. Come in at any time. I'll show you your rooms.''

Gregory gave me that anguished look that said he wanted to do whatever I wanted to do. The fact was that the only person I knew at Princeton was Sandra Simpson, who had graduated from Whitman the year before. She'd invited us to a party that night and said I could sleep in her dorm, but I wasn't sure she had room for Gregory. ''You really don't mind when we get in?'' I asked. ''I mean, it might not be late at all, but—''

''As Tate will tell you, I could sleep through a nuclear explosion,'' Pablo said.

Gregory reached out and pumped Pablo's hand. ''This really is very generous of you, Mr. Rodríguez.''

The four guest bedrooms were all on one floor, and each had two beds. The bathroom was in the hall. "However you wish to arrange this is fine with me," Pablo said, setting my bag down in the hall. "Come down when you're ready."

I picked up my bag and carried it into the front bedroom, which was lovely, with white walls and old Audubon prints of birds. I started unpacking as Gregory stood uncertainly in the doorway, holding his suitcase. "What do you think?" he asked, his voice quavering.

"Whatever you want," I said. Why was I so mean to Gregory? Was I a secret sadist, who had just never had the chance to practice before? Or did having power over someone make me nervous?

He swallowed, his eyes on my underwear as I folded it neatly and put it in the top drawer. "Well, I'd like to share a room with you," he said, "but just so we could be together. I don't want you to feel pressured."

Deciding to be magnanimous, I gave him a big smile. "Great," I said. "I'm told I talk in my sleep."

"I snore sometimes."

I suddenly wondered if Gregory, like me, had gone to a drugstore and bought some condoms. If so, we would have enough between us for several orgies. Of course, I couldn't face our friendly family druggist, Mr. Mantley, who had filled our prescriptions for years. Not because I was afraid he would tell my parents. I just preferred the anonymity of the big, gaudy People's Drugstore that had just opened across the street, which my father was afraid might drive poor Mr. Mantley out of business. I had the condoms in my cosmetics case, and I decided not to unpack them now, with Gregory watching me so avidly.

Pablo showed us the art museum he was director of and took us on a tour of the campus. "A lovely spot, charming students . . ."

"You don't have to teach them," Mr. O'Reilly pointed out dyspeptically. "So they appear charming."

"They help out at the museum. Some are charming, some are not. What can one expect?" He smiled at us—we were

74

in the back of the car. "Tate loves searching for the worm in the apple."

"Since we live in the Big Apple," Mr. O'Reilly said, "I've had a lot of practice. There are plenty of worms."

They dropped us off in front of the Princeton library, where we ran into someone Gregory had been a camp counselor with in Vermont. He was a junior and took us back to his dorm, where we met his roommate, who was about to set off for a semester in London. Gregory's friend, Monty, was pre-med, which wasn't much use to either of us, but he was a voluble, relaxed person and told us a lot about things apart from courses. His roommate, Read, had changed his major three times and was a transfer from Haverford. "I'm miserable everywhere," he said cheerfully. "I'll probably even be miserable in London. Don't go by me."

They asked what we were interested in. I said I was thinking of being an English professor. Gregory mentioned something about prelaw; neither of us mentioned writing poetry. "The English major's good," Read said. "Forget lit. It's all analyzing theories of theories. You never even get to talk about the books."

When we left Monty's room, I asked Gregory why he hadn't mentioned his poetry.

"Why didn't you?" he countered.

"Well, at least I said I was going to major in English—I wasn't denying my whole existence."

Gregory looked away. "I may be a businessman or a lawyer," he said. "Look at Wallace Stevens, or Auchincloss. Maybe it's better to be something real."

I turned on him fiercely, though of course I agreed with him as much as I disagreed. "How is poetry not real? How can you even *think* of writing it if that's how you really feel?"

Gregory looked pained. "I want to earn a living," he said coldly. "I may have a family to support, you know."

"Oh pardon me," I said. "I'll just slop around, writing the odd poem while taking clothes out of the dryer, but you—"

Gregory reached for my hand and squeezed it so hard I winced. "No," he said. "You know that's not what I meant.

It's just that you're not detached from reality the way I am. Women never are. You don't need that extra thing. And I wasn't suggesting you'd do nothing. Is teaching college nothing?''

I was winding down. "I am *so* detached from reality," I said. "That's not a male prerogative."

"You have friends," he said. "You always have. Men friends, women friends . . . I'm a hopeless loner."

I hated it when Gregory got into his self-pitying mood, even though I was familiar with it myself. "Well, at least now you have me," I said with a wry smile.

The party that night had a theme. Everyone was to go as the contraceptive device of his or her choice. Sandra was going as the rhythm method, with a calendar stitched onto her black, floor-length dress. Since we were guests, we could come as we were. When Gregory brought me a drink, some lethal-tasting punch, I said, "I don't think we should stick together all evening. We'll learn more if we talk to people separately. Then we can compare notes later."

He looked woebegone for a moment. I didn't really mean I intended to try to pick men up at the party, just that I was afraid if we spent the entire evening together, my decision to devirginize both of us might begin to unravel. Actually, I ended up spending most of the party talking to a girl, Lona, who was a freshman and having a miserable time at the party, as well as at Princeton. "It's probably me," she said. "I'm from Ohio. I'm a hick. . . . And everyone says freshman year is awful. Don't judge by me."

It turned out, though, that she wrote poetry and she thought her best course was a poetry seminar. "That's what I live for—the rest is shit."

When I told her I wrote poetry too, she reached into her huge bag, and drew out some of her poems. We went into a corner and sat cross-legged on the floor, where she read to me by candlelight.

At midnight I looked around for Gregory.

"Is that your boyfriend?" Lona asked, squinting across the room with me at Gregory, who appeared to be having an animated discussion with an extremely pretty, dark-haired

76

girl who wore her hair in one of those complicated French braids I'd always admired.

"Sort of," I said. "I can't decide."

"It looks like he can't either," she said dryly. Then she added, "Every guy here has a high school girlfriend they drag out the second they're afraid you're getting involved."

"Oh, we're not really . . ." But I was too tired to try to explain my relationship with Gregory, which would have meant explaining my relationship with Stuart, and then we might have been there all night. I excused myself and sauntered over to claim Gregory. I tapped him on the shoulder. "Hi," I said. "Remember me?"

"Oh, Isabel . . . I didn't know where you'd gone. This is Topaz. She's prelaw and is interested in writing."

Topaz was even prettier close up than she'd seemed across the room. "Don't come here for men," she advised me. "This is the first good conversation I've had with a man since I got here. They're mostly useless."

"I don't think I'll come here at all," I said coldly. I didn't feel jealous, but somehow irritated. Looking up at Gregory, I said, "I'm tired. Maybe we should go back."

I leaned against him seductively.

Despite this, Topaz gave him a good-bye kiss and promised to "stay in touch."

As we strolled back to Pablo's house, Gregory, his arm around me, said, "She was so nice! Girls like that usually never talk to me. I think just being with you, knowing I came to the party with you, makes me more self-confident."

"Why does anyone name a child Topaz?" I asked. It was very quiet and cold on the street, but windless. Topaz reminded me of Chester's ex-girlfriend, Amber.

"Yet it sort of suited her," Gregory said. "She had a kind of glow. . . . I mean, basically I agree with you. *I'd* never name a child Topaz." I was almost afraid he was going to say "our child."

"The girls here seem to be desperate for men," I said meanly.

But Gregory just answered with a smile, "Yeah, I guess it would be a great place to go, from that point of view."

Pablo had left the front door unlocked, as he had said he would. We tiptoed up to the second floor and silently closed the door to our room. "Do you think they're lovers?" Gregory whispered.

"I would guess, though they seem so different."

"True, but who would have guessed that you'd choose me?" At my stricken, or anxious, face, he added, "Oh, I didn't mean . . . I mean, as far as tonight goes, we definitely don't have to—"

"No, let's," I said firmly. "I think we should. I think we owe it to ourselves." I took the condoms out of my cosmetics case. "I have these," I said.

Gregory beamed. "That's so . . . thoughtful. I brought some too, actually. The same kind. I guess it doesn't matter which ones we use."

VIRGINS

The fact that we were both nervous, self-conscious virgins was a help. I regarded this as something to be gotten through, and if one second of it was enjoyable, that would be a pleasant surprise. I raced through my usual bedtime ritual and was in bed, naked, while Gregory was still brushing his teeth. I didn't know if he always did everything slowly or if his slowness was like my speed, a reaction to the awkward situation. I felt lucky, being undressed but under the covers, while he had to undress with me watching. Of course, I could have closed my eyes or looked away, but I was curious, and it was almost like watching a striptease, he went so slowly, hanging everything on hangers, even. When he was down to his underpants, he slid into bed next to me and removed them under the covers, so I missed the part I'd been waiting for.

Gregory was freezing cold. Mainly it was that his hands and feet, his extremities (not to pun), were so cold that every time he tried to put a hand on even my stomach, say, I'd let out a yelp. It was like having an ice cube dropped down your dress. Each time I yelped, he'd draw back, sure he had done something wrong or gone too far. "Why don't we kiss for a

79

long time," he suggested. "At least we know we can do that. . . . And there's no law saying we have to do anything else."

"There is," I said. "It's a law that only applies in the state of New Jersey, and it dates back to the days of the Puritans." But I agreed. We both loved to kiss, and we were good at it, long, sloppy, intense kisses, which is what we did for a half hour at least, almost afraid to move our hands anywhere they hadn't previously been allowed to go. I'd been afraid it would be painful when he tried to enter my body, but by the time he got around to that, it wasn't. He just slid in. Evidently nature's lubricant worked on its own, regardless of nervousness or doubt that I was really in love, or doing it with the "right person." The other disaster I'd feared was that Gregory wouldn't be able to get an erection or, if he did, would lose it in the middle. That didn't happen either. He got an erection early on, while we were kissing, and it never went away.

That, actually, was the problem. I'd been prepared for the entire act to take only about three seconds, so I decided at first not to even try and have an orgasm. I expected Gregory to come in one second, and collapse apologetically on my breast, promising that next time it would take longer, and be better. But after five or six minutes—it seemed like hours, actually—it occurred to me I would have time, and I might as well at least try, so I did, and it worked. Of course I'd had orgasms while masturbating, but I'd read all sorts of statistics about how many women never did during intercourse at all. I was floored at hitting the jackpot the first time. Maybe I was going to turn out to be a nymphomaniac after all; maybe there'd be no stopping me! But Gregory was still thrusting back and forth. "Did you come?" I asked, thinking maybe he had come but didn't think I had, and this could go on all night.

"No," he said despairingly, "and I'm not going to."

"How do you know?" I said. "Just relax. We have all night." Though the idea of doing it all night was stupefying, to say the least.

"Doesn't it hurt?" he asked.

"No, not really, not at all," I lied. Now I was engaged in an act of charity, not one of erotic dalliance. It just wouldn't be fair for me to fall asleep while Gregory tossed and turned, filled with mortification and self-hatred. So we went on. I thought I might try for another orgasm, but by then the sense of Gregory's desperation had infected me.

Finally he withdrew and lay on his back, his arm over his eyes. "This is typical," he said. "I *knew* this would happen."

"You mean something going wrong, or this in particular?"

"I knew I'd fuck up somehow." He laughed hollowly. "I mean, how many men in the United States, in the *world*, even, would, when you put them in bed with a sweet, pretty, sexy girl whom they're in love with, not even be able to do it. It must be like minus a thousand percent!"

I sighed. My head was on his shoulder. "I haven't had any experience," I said. "There are probably lots of things I should have done that might've made the difference." Though, frankly, I couldn't think of any.

"What if this is symbolic of my whole life?" Gregory moaned. "What if I turn out to be like my father? He can only get really turned on by call girls. That's why he goes to them. Women he respects . . . Oh God, that's the worst thing in the world I can think of, being like my father, the absolute worst!"

"You're *not* like your father," I promised him. "You're nervous, that's all it is. I mean, you gave me an orgasm, and think how rare that is the first time. So it proves your technique is fantastic. Maybe I'm too known," I said, "or too detached. Maybe if you'd gone home with Amber—"

"Who's Amber?" Gregory asked.

"I mean Topaz," I corrected myself.

"The girl at the party? But she wouldn't have gone home with me," Gregory said. "Not in a million years."

"Sure she would." I was getting so used to lying, it was becoming fun. After all, we were talking about a hypothetical situation. "I could tell even looking at her across the room."

Gregory sighed with pleasure and squeezed my hand. "She did seem to be coming on a little," he said. "But I thought it was because she'd had too much to drink."

"Drink only makes you reveal things you'd normally feel but would be afraid to show," I said.

"And she knew about you," Gregory said. "I told her I was in love with you. Do you mind? So she couldn't have—"

I did mind, horribly, but it didn't, under the circumstances, seem worth going into. "That might have been a kind of stimulus," I said. "It is for some girls. . . . All I'm saying is I'm one kind of person, and this is one time. You can't generalize from just one time. We could even try it again in a few minutes." The idea exhausted me emotionally as well as physically, but luckily Gregory said, "No, you know what, let's just go to sleep now. You've made me feel good, and it's not like this is our only chance. I mean, back in the city we can always . . . if you want . . . If you don't want, of course I'd understand."

I reached over and kissed him. "Of course I'll want." Having a good sound sleep sounded wonderful, a reprieve from the effort of erotic ups or downs. "Sweet dreams."

Gregory and I both slept like logs. He didn't even snore, or if he did, I was too deeply asleep to hear him. When I woke up I went in to shower and came out clean, aware that I was a little sore, but not feeling bad at all. I looked at him sleeping, like a male Sleeping Beauty whom I had somehow not managed to quite drag with me into the field of nonvirginity. Or had I? I began wondering about that as I got dressed. Was a man still a virgin if he'd "done it" but hadn't ejaculated? It sounded like a question one would never think to ask in sex ed.

Slowly Gregory's eyes opened. When he saw me, he looked as I imagined he would have looked if everything had gone perfectly. I went over and he pulled me down and kissed me. "You're a darling," he said.

I didn't know if that meant I should undress and we should start all over, but he bounded out of bed and said, "That smells like cornbread and bacon. Great!"

"The shower's good too," I said. "A lot of pressure."
Everything suddenly seemed to have a double meaning.
Should I go downstairs alone or wait for Gregory? I was a
little afraid if I went downstairs with him, it would seem
incriminating. But what else would they expect to have happened? Or maybe they truly didn't care, the way my father
wouldn't have. When Gregory came out of the shower, I
said, "I'm hungry too. Do you mind if I go down for breakfast?"

He was naked, dripping wet, but I caught a glimpse of
what I'd missed the night before, and it looked fine, not that
I had any point of comparison. I couldn't recall ever seeing
my father undressed. But once, when Lois and I were eight,
we were in a rowboat at camp with a male counselor named
Winnie, who exposed himself to us as he was rowing. Lois
and I were at one end of the rowboat, facing Winnie, and
neither of us knew the meaning of the term "indecent exposure," or even that that was what was happening. We
thought his penis had happened to "fall" out, which explained why he had such a funny, embarrassed look on his
face. We tried delicately to look away, thinking it might give
him the opportunity to stuff it back in, but he never did. For
the rest of the summer we felt terribly sorry for him. To us,
it was the grown-up equivalent of wetting your bed at camp
and having your sheets hung out to dry where everyone could
see.

Downstairs Pablo was bustling around in the kitchen.
"How do you like your eggs?" he asked. "Soft, medium,
scrambled?"

"Scrambled would be great . . . but I can do it."

"Nonsense," Pablo said. "I make incredible scrambled
eggs. Even if you decide not to go to Princeton, at least you'll
have had my scrambled eggs, and that will have made the
trip worthwhile." He began whipping some up in a small
copper bowl.

"Where's Mr. O'Reilly?" I asked, looking around.

"He's gone for a walk. What an impossible man! I'm sure
he is a wonderful teacher, but he never eats properly. I've
shown him dozens of articles on how dangerous it is to go

83

without a decent breakfast and he ignores it. . . . Rye toast or cornbread?''

"Cornbread, please." He slid a platter of eggs and bacon in front of me. There was one of those glass jars divided into compartments with different kinds of jams that I'd only seen at inns. "Gregory will be down in a minute," I said, my mouth full.

"Let him sleep. . . . Did you find the beds comfortable?''

I blushed. "Yes, extremely." Then after a second I added, "It was so nice of you to put us up.''

"I love it, I love guests. . . . It's probably from growing up in a large family. Noise stimulates me." He was sipping some viciously strong-looking black coffee. "You're the poet, I gather?''

"Well, we both are," I said. "Gregory writes poetry too.''

"But I understood from what Tate said, you— He just didn't happen to mention your friend. He's that way. Each year, or every few years, there's one student . . . He calls them his imaginary children." His big eyes sparkled mischievously.

"I know," I said.

"A lot cheaper and less messy than real ones," Pablo said. "Not that I'd know. I don't have either kind. But I have so many nieces and nephews, it amounts to the same thing. Six sisters, and they all married before they were twenty. I can hardly keep track of them.''

I was sipping my coffee in a gingerly way. "I'm not sure I want children," I said.

I was expecting him, like most people, to argue with me, but he just said, "Why should you? There'll always be plenty of people around who do, or who have them anyway. One needn't worry about that.''

"One needn't worry about what?" Gregory asked as he came bounding into the room.

"Isabel and I were discussing the nonnecessity of having children," Pablo said.

"I want four," Gregory said firmly.

Pablo was back at the stove. "Eggs?''

"Oh . . . no, just two, please, scrambled. No, I meant I want four children." He beamed at me as though we'd gotten

84

engaged the night before and were, like Hal and Andria, into skimming through name-your-baby books.

"Then you'll have to marry some sort of lobotomized workhorse of a woman," I said, "who turns out babies until she collapses in a heap." I had just read *Parallel Lives*, a book with fascinating portraits of Victorian marriages, and was struck by the horrifying account of Dickens's marriage.

"But then he can leave her for a lithesome young thing and get joint custody, or have the children on vacations," Pablo said, setting a plate in front of Gregory.

"But the second wife will want children herself," I argued. "She'll be in her twenties or thirties, and will force him to have a whole second lot, even though by then he'll be fifty-two and struggling to pay college tuition for the first four."

"Oh, but by then Wife One will have found herself," Pablo intervened. "She'll have become a lawyer or started her own business or something, and she'll be filled with menopausal zeal. Women always are in their fifties, just as men are beginning to burn out. It's one of nature's many nasty little jokes."

Gregory was simultaneously eating furiously and looking at the two of us in horror. "How awful," he said finally. "Stop! That's *not* what I want at all. I'm going to marry one woman, and I'm going to love her faithfully and devotedly all my life."

Pablo arched an eyebrow and raised his coffee cup as though it were a champagne glass. "Good luck," he said.

Mr. O'Reilly returned to find us sitting silently at the breakfast table. "Been discussing poetry?" he asked mildly.

"Larger things," Pablo said. "Life, marriage, destiny, children . . ."

"Larger?" Mr. O'Reilly said. "That sounds minuscule. . . . Well, little ones, have you seen all there is to see of this estimable establishment?"

"I'd like to take a last walk through the campus," Gregory said. "Could we leave in three quarters of an hour?"

"We can leave at any time, at any hour," Mr. O'Reilly

said. He shook his head. "Shame on you, Pablo. Stuffing these innocents with cholesterol-laden food. Their arteries!"

"They're babies," Pablo said. "They have no arteries." He began clearing up.

"Can I help?" I asked.

"Off on your walk," he commanded. "This one needs to earn his keep," and, amazingly, he tied an apron around Mr. O'Reilly's waist and faced him toward the sink. Even more amazingly, Mr. O'Reilly just smiled and waved us off.

Gregory and I had a long, bracing walk. It was cold but very sunny, so much so that Gregory put on a pair of sunglasses and leather gloves. "They must be lovers," he said.

"Why?" I asked, wondering if people, seeing us, thought the same thing, if there was some way you could tell.

"The apron," Gregory said. "That was a dead give-away. . . . But really, Isabel, I think you *should* have children. Not with me, necessarily. But with someone. I mean, you can write as well."

"On the side?" I said sarcastically, thinking of those dismissive references to "housewife writer" I had seen in reviews of books by women writers.

"No," he said, taking my hand. "You'll have *children* on the side."

"I'm not that conventional," I said. His leather-clad hand was warming; my fingers were freezing. "I don't want a conventional life."

"Conventional doesn't mean boring," Gregory said.

The fact was that even though our attempt at losing our virginity might be deemed less than a roaring success, we both felt good about it, and pleased with ourselves and each other. I didn't mind if people saw Gregory holding my hand and assumed we were lovers. I just wasn't sure we were. Finally, on the way back to Pablo's house, I asked him. "Are we not virgins anymore?"

Obviously Gregory had been thinking of that too. "Well, you're certainly not," he said. "Isn't it penetration that counts as far as the woman goes?"

I started giggling. "I guess. . . . But you were the penetrator—is that a word?"

86

"I think it's penetrant, actually," Gregory said.

"It seems to have fallen into disuse," I said. "But even so . . . I think we both aren't. I suppose it doesn't matter so much to a man."

Gregory dropped my hand. "Of course it matters! I think it matters a lot more."

"Oh, you mean in the sense that you've scored, as it were, *you've* gained something, and I've *lost* something?"

"No, I *don't* mean that. I think we've *both* gained something . . . don't you?" He looked desperately anxious for my approval.

"Yes, definitely."

We walked on in silence.

"I'm so glad you had an orgasm," Gregory said suddenly. "I mean, it's to your credit, but—"

"No, I'm glad too," I admitted. "I didn't expect to. And it's to your credit too."

I wasn't sure how big a role credit played in this. But just as we couldn't help, even the morning after, being our self-conscious intellectual selves, we couldn't help being happy at being among the haves, rather than the have-nots. Or maybe it was the other way around, if virginity was the thing we both no longer had.

"DON'T SIGH
AND GAZE AT ME"

I wasn't sure whether to tell anyone. Even though I'd done it in some way to get back at Stuart because of Ketti, I didn't want him to know. I wanted it to be my secret, and I'd warned Gregory sternly not to gaze at me adoringly in the halls at school, like that song from *Oklahoma*, "Don't sigh and gaze at me . . . People will say we're in love." I didn't even know if we *were* in love, but whatever we were in, I wanted it not to be public property, especially among the "fearsome foursome," who were ten times more eagle-eyed than my mother.

Staring at myself naked in the mirror, looking deep into my eyes, I was convinced that I looked exactly the same. I had no sudden desire to wear skintight jeans, or flirt with anonymous strangers. I just carried the secret around with me like a prize at the bottom of a Cracker Jack box, examining it occasionally. The person I most wanted to tell was Lois. Her comments, I was sure, would be special, not just "Well, finally" or "Was it great?" But I kept putting it off.

Then, two weeks after our visit to Princeton, Lois and her father invited me to dinner and the theater. After the theater Miller retreated to his study to read. Lois and I made cocoa, as we always did, and brought the mugs back to her bedroom. It was late, she looked sleepy, and I wasn't sure if I should tell her about Gregory, now or ever. We brushed our teeth, I got into bed first, she turned off the lights. The beds were across from each other, a few feet apart. "Sweet dreams," Lois said.

"You too." After a moment I blurted out, "I slept with Gregory."

"What?"

I repeated what I'd said.

Lois sat up in bed. She turned on the light. "Are you kidding?"

I flinched. "Turn it off."

"I want to see if you're telling the truth. . . . Look me in the eye and tell me."

I did. "Now could you turn the light off?"

After she clicked off the light, there was a deadly silence. I felt terrible. "How do you feel about it?" I asked.

"Awful! . . . . I just can't *believe* it. Why would you do it? Just to be like them? To have some stupid little secret to boast about at school? That's sick."

"That wasn't why," I said, crushed. Lois was usually so quiet, so unemphatic.

"Gregory Arrington! He doesn't even write good poetry!"

"Well, it's not really bad. . . . But really, Lo, he's a nice person. He's got a lot of hidden depth." How could I stoop so low?

"How did it happen? Did you seduce him? Like in the play?" We'd seen *Les Liaisons Dangereuses*.

"No." I told her about the weekend. "It just seemed to happen naturally."

"You bought *condoms*? I can't believe it! I absolutely can't."

"Just to be on the safe side. I didn't know it would happen."

"You did! You knew if you bought them, you'd use them."

"I didn't know he'd want to," I said lamely.

"Isabel, this is so unlike you! Of *course* you knew he'd

89

want to. He's been mooning at you for weeks! He's the laughingstock of the whole school.''

"Why?" I felt hurt. "For liking me?"

"No, for being that open about it, for acting like such a jerk. . . . But no one thought *you* were taking *him* seriously."

I, of course, had had all these same inner debates in my head. "He is not a jerk," I said angrily, hurt. "What's all that terrible about showing your feelings? That's what I *like* about him. It isn't game playing. It's real."

"Real *what*? Real love?"

Her voice was so contemptuous, so scathing, that I wanted to crawl into a hole. "I don't know." I wavered, glad of the protection of the dark. "We care for each other. It's a million things. I did, somehow, want not to be a virgin anymore. Is that so terrible?"

"Yes." There was a pause. "Anyway, you weren't."

"What do you mean?"

"You did it with me," she said in a quavering voice. "Or don't you remember that?"

"Of course I remember," I said softly. "I just—"

"—thought that only doing it with a guy was what counted. What *we* did didn't count. It was just some stupid preadolescent junk.''

Suddenly I got out of bed and went and knelt beside Lois's bed. She was crying. "Lo, really. I love you, seriously. I just don't think I'm gay. I really don't. It's not like I'm putting this on some higher plane."

Lois was sobbing openly now. "Now you're a normal person," she wept. "How can we be friends?"

"I'm *not* a normal person," I said, stroking her shoulder. "I'll never be, will you believe me? And Gregory isn't normal either. He's just like us. He's insecure and self-doubting. That's what I *like* about him. . . . And it wasn't even . . .''

I told her about what it had really been like.

She stopped sobbing and sniffed. "So, he has, like, sexual problems?''

"I don't know. It was just the once. I think eventually he'll get the hang of it." Poor Gregory. I hadn't meant to be quite this clinical about our encounter.

"You're going to keep doing it till you get it right? You're a couple now?" But her sarcasm was more muted.

"No. Definitely not. I'm telling you, and no one else. Please don't tell the others. I don't want anyone but you to know."

"Not even Stuart?" Lois asked acutely.

I was silent, watching the digital hand on her clock flick from 1:23 to 1:24. "I don't know."

Suddenly Lois reached over and hugged me. "God, I'm such a fool. Why are you friends with me? Will you forgive me?"

"Of course. . . . I'd probably have felt the same way if *you'd* done it with anyone." Though I doubted it. I climbed back into bed, feeling exhausted but better.

"I always thought if you were going to do it with a guy, you'd do it with Stuart first," Lois said thoughtfully.

I stared at the ceiling. "He has Ketti."

"That's just a passing fling."

"You think?"

"Sure. He's not her type, really."

After a moment Lois asked, "Could you see eventually getting around to enjoying it, just physically, I mean?"

"Yeah," I admitted ruefully. "I really could."

AN EMBARRASSMENT OF RICHES

I did break down and write some love poems, which I showed to Mr. O'Reilly in the weeks before Christmas vacation. He read through them with evident distaste. "What does this have to do with your senior project?" he asked.

"Does *everything* have to do with that?" I asked.

"These are squandering of your time. They're banal, in subject, in language. . . . How *could* you, Isabel?"

"Did you actually read them?" I was more angry than hurt.

He leafed dismissively through the sheets. "I read the first, I glanced at the others. You've read Elizabeth Barrett Browning, haven't you?"

"Of course."

"Let her be a lesson to you. That's what happens when lady poets end up slithering around in great pools of undigested erotic feeling."

I pretended to be taken aback. "*Lady* poets?"

"Yes, and I don't mean her sexual identity. I mean, slosh!" His face was red, his voice was shaking.

"How about Shakespeare's sonnets?" I fired back.

"Even those. . . . I'm sorry, I know you'll disagree, but men just don't— They control the emotion a bit more, some-how."

"It must be hormonal," I said coldly.

"It must be. . . . But frankly, even Shakespeare did far *far* better when he directed his attentions elsewhere."

"Romeo and Juliet?" We had studied that in sophomore year.

"Horribly overrated. Laughable in so many ways. Mercutio steals the play, and once he's gone, who cares, really, if they make it together or not. I mean, *Lear* is *intrinsically* a tragedy, down to its very bones. Even if Cordelia hadn't died at the end. . . . Whereas Romeo and Juliet could just as well have hopped off to Venice and set up housekeeping, and she could have had a dozen kids—"

"And died in childbirth at thirty," I put in.

"And he would have remarried at least twice. Yes, that's the point," Mr. O'Reilly said. "Not that there's anything new to be said about anything. We agree about that. But the subject of love is one about which there never *was* anything to be said. When I see those graffiti in the men's room, 'X loves Y,' I think cavemen probably etched those on the walls of their caves and said it all."

"I think it's important to try writing about things one may write badly about," I said, repeating back to him one of his own theories.

Mr. O'Reilly raised an eyebrow. "Could you spare *me* then? Write them by all means, and show them to your fellow sufferer, or your girlfriends, but I want to preserve my image of you as someone with an intellect, not simply a mass of organs sloshing around."

I laughed. "You're wonderful," I said.

Mr. O'Reilly looked surprised. "Am I? What a frightening thought."

Both Lois and Gregory kept their word. At school Gregory kept his ardent glances to a minimum, and Lois never told anyone. Even when we met one day at Ketti's house, and Andria asked with a sly smile how my weekend at Princeton with Gregory had gone, I just said, "I don't think either of us will go there."

She shook her head. "That wasn't what I meant."

"We were as chaste as doves."

"How come?" Ketti said. "He's pining for you. Didn't you have a chance?"

"We did," I said. "We shared the same room, actually." I told them about Pablo and Mr. O'Reilly. "But we got back from the party kind of trashed, and . . . I don't know. Nothing happened. The story of my life."

"Would you tell us if something had?" Andria asked cannily.

"Sure," I lied effortlessly.

Andria was knitting a long, multicolored scarf. "I guess I feel sorry for poor old Gregory. He's not bad looking."

Ketti was lying on her back, gazing at the ceiling. "He *is* kind of a loser, though. Admit it."

"He's *not* a loser," Lois said sweetly, coming to my defense, knowing I couldn't.

"I agree," Andria said. "I bet the right woman could turn him into a tiger. . . . How's it going with Stuart, Kett? Speaking of—"

My heart plummeted in that sick way. I looked at her. She smiled tantalizingly. "Oh, Stuart's a darling," she said.

"Yeah?" Andria said. "So, come on, give us the gory details."

"There's nothing gory. He's tender and caring. He may be a little flabby compared to some, but I really like his way of doing things." She glanced at me. "You were right, Iz. I might not have thought of him if you hadn't mentioned it, but I'm glad you did. He's not my ultimate type, and I'm not his, but for now it's perfect."

Lois, I knew, was looking at me keenly. "Great," I said with false cheer. "Why isn't he your type, though? How about opposites attract?"

Ketti was really pretty, with her tawny blond hair falling just far enough into her eyes so she had to toss it back, or run her fingers through it. "I guess, even though he likes to horse around, I think Stuart is really the serious type."

94

I don't know what I'd hoped might happen, now that my "suggestion" that Ketti and Stuart get together had become a reality. One version of my sadistic fantasies was that Stuart would fall horribly for Ketti, would suffer anguish while she treated him like a dog—but that backfired, even in fantasy, because I didn't want to see Stuart moping around in love in the way Mr. O'Reilly had such contempt for. The other fantasy was that Ketti would fall head over heels for Stuart, and would make such a pest of herself that he would have to come to me for advice on how to get rid of her. That seemed improbable, somehow.

Anyway, I felt I had to follow through with Gregory. It wasn't fair to go to bed with him once and leave him hanging, especially when it had gone the way it had. The problem, as it is for all city kids, was finding a place. I gather in the suburbs kids do it in cars, and in the country they do it in fields or barns. We had to find a vacant apartment. The trouble was my parents never went away. One afternoon I went over to ask Olive's advice.

"I'm seeing someone," I explained, "and it's a little awkward because we have no place to go."

Olive was looking tired, but in that feminine, soft way she had. "Is it serious?"

"I don't know," I said. "We haven't had much chance to—"

"It's so hard to tell with men," she mused. "Impossible, really. I ought to be an expert by now, but the plain fact of the matter is you don't know until you get there. I wish it were otherwise."

I got a thrill out of Olive's being willing to confide in me. It seemed so different from sitting around with the foursome, trading notes. Olive never seemed boasting, or flip, and yet I knew no other adult who would take me seriously enough to consider me worthy of confidences. To my mother the whole topic was taboo, and to my father it seemed almost not to exist. Maybe if I'd had an older sister, or a girl cousin, I could have talked with her the way I did with Olive, but I didn't.

"I know I'm not in love with Jerry," Olive said, "though

I'm not sure why. I hope I'm not becoming cautious the way everyone does at my age. I truly don't think it's that. With Chester I just fell head over heels, and I don't know if I've really ever recovered from that. Maybe I never will."

Her eyes were a lovely bluish-green. Once I tried green contacts at the eye doctor's, to see if I could look catlike, like Olive, but I didn't. "He'd love to get back with you," I said. "All he does is talk about you."

Olive smiled ruefully. "Yes, I can imagine."

"Don't you believe him? Don't you think it's genuine?"

"Oh, I do. . . . No one's ever broken your heart, Isabel, and so you don't know. It's banal, and idiotic, but once done, it can't be repaired."

"But he did it with someone he didn't love," I said, trying to defend Chester. "And he was so young, and it was just the one time."

"I know," Olive said. "You're perfectly right, and the fact is I've done things like that myself, and I'm not a moralistic person. It's just there's something in me that cracked, that won't mend. And Jerry is just right for now, because he won't get anywhere near that part of me."

I felt terribly sad. I wanted Olive to be intensely, passionately in love, the way she had been in the early Chester days when she was so luminous and radiant that I would stare at her in awe.

"To get back to you," she said. "Jerry and I *are* planning a trip to Washington in a week or two, and surely Stuart can stay with Katherine the Great." (That was always her way of referring to Ketti.)

"Could you not tell him?" I asked, suddenly anxious.

"Oh, Jerry doesn't mind at all," Olive said. "He—"

"I meant, could you not tell Stuart? Is there any way you could—"

Olive looked at me curiously. "Why?" she asked.

I shrugged. "I don't know. I guess I . . . It's just that in our school, once someone knows, everyone knows."

"Stuart's not a gossip," Olive said. "And you've been friends such a long time. I'm sure if you asked him not to tell, he wouldn't."

96

"I don't *want* to ask him," I blurted out. I felt so desperate on this subject, I wished I hadn't brought it up. "Listen, Olive, actually, we may not need the apartment at all. We may—"

At that moment Stuart walked in, whistling breezily. Maybe my anxious expression, or the sudden silence that greeted him, tipped him off. "Anyone die that I don't know about?" he asked.

"Isabel and I were just talking about life," Olive said.

Stuart looked properly suspicious. "That's got to be a euphemism for something. Fucking? Isabel doesn't approve of it. She only writes about it."

"You're so nasty, Stu," Olive said. "Apologize."

Unexpectedly Stuart got down on bended knee and seized my hand, kissing it. "Wilt thou forgive me, fairest Isabel?"

I sighed. "You're hopeless . . . you're beyond hope. Do you know that?"

"I do. . . . Will you?"

"I will."

"To be continued," Olive said to me, winking.

Stuart whistled. "Boy, does *that* sound incriminating! What are you two doing—planning some little orgy behind my back? The minute I'm out of sight—"

"Were you planning on going anywhere?" Olive asked quickly.

"Ketti and I thought of maybe going to Boston in a week or so. For our Harvard interviews."

"Ketti at Harvard?" Olive said disdainfully.

"Her chances are a lot better than mine," Stuart said.

"Hormones talking," Olive said.

"No, he's right. She *is* awfully bright," I said. "Maybe you'll both get in, and then your whatever can go right on."

Stuart was rummaging in the refrigerator. "No, our whatever will come to a skidding and agreed-upon halt on June seventh."

"Why then?" Olive asked.

"Graduation," Stuart said. "Then we go on to greener pastures." He was munching on a pear. "Though I must admit, Ketti's pastures are pretty damn green."

97

The two weekends did come together: Jerry and Olive in Washington, Ketti and Stuart in Boston. Then it turned out Gregory's parents were going away Friday night. "An embarrassment of riches," he said on the phone. "Which will it be?"

"Which night, you mean?"

"Which apartment."

I knew I would feel far less at ease at Olive and Stuart's— it was almost like home. "Maybe yours would be better."

That Friday we went to a movie and came back at nearly midnight. To our horror, when we opened the front door, Gregory's parents were in the kitchen. His father was very tall, very fat, and totally bald. His mother was tiny and unhappy looking, with oddly punkish white hair, almost as close cropped as a boy's, and big, sad, dark eyes, like Gregory's. He clearly got his height from his father and his angst from his mother. "Hi," Gregory said. "This is Isabel."

"The famed Isabel," Mr. Arrington said. "Welcome. You must be starving. I'm about to make one of my famous ice-cream fruit drinks. Care to try one?"

"What's in it?" I asked.

"It's a secret recipe," he said. "A bunch of strawberries, a teaspoon of vanilla. It will taste very much like a milk shake, but about a million times better."

"I thought you guys were going to visit the Schneiders," Gregory said, leaning against the refrigerator, which was about as tall as he was. It was a high-tech kitchen, all in chrome and white, with ominous-looking food machines everywhere.

"She's sick again," Mrs. Arrington said in a soft, hoarse whisper. "It's such a pity. Last week she seemed so well."

I knew what Gregory was feeling, but I couldn't decide what I was feeling. Relief? Now I'd been let off the hook and could go home to a good book? No, I'd told my parents I was staying at Lois's. But I could say she was sick. Mulling all this over, I took the ice-cream punch automatically and drank it in almost one gulp.

Mr. Arrington watched me in horror. "You must have been terribly thirsty," he said. "It's meant to be sipped."

98

"Oh," I said vaguely. "I'm sorry."

Gregory beckoned me into his room. It was large and messy, except for his desk, which had neat stacks of papers on both sides of a large word processor. I had never thought of writing poetry on a word processor. Maybe he used it for term papers. "Shit," he said, punching his fist on the desk. "I could *kill* them."

"It's Mrs. Schneider," I pointed out. "They couldn't go if she was sick."

He looked hopeless and despairing. "I've been looking forward to this for weeks. I just can't—" His voice broke.

I was touched. "I'll tell you what," I said. "Tonight I'll go home, and you stay here."

"But you told your parents you were staying at Lois's."

"I can stay at Olive and Jerry's by myself. They're away for the weekend, and Stuart and Ketti are in Boston for their Harvard interviews."

Gregory looked delighted. "They won't mind? Do you have a key?"

"Yes, and no, they won't mind. Olive's almost like a friend, I've known her so long."

Gregory came over and put his arms around me. He had to bend down to kiss the top of my head. "I don't deserve you," he said. "You're wonderful. You make me so happy."

I felt pleased at cheering him up, and also at having one night's reprieve. "Wait until tomorrow," I said, realizing after I'd said it that it sounded different from how I'd meant it. I'd meant: You may not think I'm as wonderful tomorrow, but it sounded like he might think I was still better, that everything up to now had been previews of coming attractions.

"I'm glad you thought of that," Gregory said. "I would've hated doing it here. This place *reeks* of them. Stuart's mother's place is anonymous—it has no associations, almost like a hotel." He blushed. "You know what I mean."

I did, except, of course, it was the opposite for me. It was as far from anonymous to me as anywhere on earth.

I felt a little nervous as I got off at our floor, but it was past midnight, and I knew my parents were asleep. I let myself into Olive's apartment. It was eerily quiet, the way an empty apartment is. I had a sudden terror that Stuart and Ketti might be there, even though I knew their interviews were for Saturday, but upon opening the bedroom doors, I found only empty beds. Where should I sleep? With Gregory I would sleep in Olive's sumptuous bed. Her bedroom was flowery and sunny, a perfect room in which to make love. Whereas Stuart's had the disheveled look of an average teenage male's. But I slept in his bed that night. I had a few moments of inner debate, wondering if it was sick or perverse to like the smell of his clothes and sheets, but I was asleep in no time.

GREEN SHEETS
WITH WAVY LINES

I woke up late the next morning at ten-thirty, to the phone ringing. Somehow I hadn't thought of that. Should I answer it or not? I'd given Gregory the number, and luckily it was he.

"I was up all night," he groaned. "It was so frustrating! I kept having these incredible dreams about you, and it practically drove me crazy."

"Maybe you can take a nap this afternoon," I suggested, feeling guilty at my own dreamless sleep.

"I'm going to swim," he said. Gregory was hardly more of an athlete than Stuart, but he claimed his outlet for sexual tension was to swim fifty laps. "When do you want me?" he said.

I decided to overlook the double entendre of that comment. "I think evening is safest," I said, "in view of my parents."

"Right. . . . Well, I could bring a pizza over at seven. Didn't you say they're usually eating then?"

"Say you're visiting Stuart, if the doorman asks," I said.

"Won't he know he's not there?"

"No, they're kind of spaced out, and usually they don't even ask."

I must inherit from my father my ability to stay indoors all day and never feel at all pent up. In fact, it was a really nice day. I spent the morning snooping around Stuart's room. I knew boys almost never keep diaries, but I ransacked the room just in case. There was nothing incriminating, no little love notes from Ketti, not even a photo of her. Oddly, in his bottom desk drawer I found a photo of me at the age of two. I was sitting on a tricycle, and it was a picture that had a double exposure, so that there were two of me, one behind the other.

In the afternoon I read *As You Like It* and some of Sylvia Plath's poems for Mr. O'Reilly's class. He approved of her, because she'd been sensible enough to commit suicide; he liked violent, definitive action. "How can anyone say suicide isn't the answer to anything?" he said. "It's a perfect answer." It was always hard to tell when Mr. O'Reilly was just being outrageous.

I felt gloomy after an afternoon of reading Plath and decided to call Lois. Miller answered and said she was away at her Mount Holyoke interview. She knew I was using her as my cover. I guess she had decided just telling my parents I was staying with her was enough. I was silent. Wouldn't it have been simpler if I'd just said to my parents, "I'm no longer a virgin. I'll be away for the weekend with my boyfriend, who is as honest and respectable as they come," and left it at that? It *would* have been simpler, but it would also have been impossible.

"Isabel," Miller said, "are you still there?"

"Yes," I said. "Sorry, I was just thinking."

"Is there a problem?" he asked gently.

For some reason I trusted Miller. He had some of my father's impassivity, but with a greater worldliness. I told him the problem.

"Say no more," he said. "You're here if they call. I'm planning to spend the evening in."

"That's so nice of you," I gushed, really meaning it. "It's amazing you can be so understanding."

"Amazing? Do I seem like an old-fashioned brute of a father? Is that the rumor Lois has been spreading about me?"

"No, it's just—"

"Have a lovely evening, Isabel."

"Thank you," I said. I hung up, wondering if he thought this was the first time for me, if he had ever suspected about me and Lois, if he would care if he knew.

Gregory arrived promptly at seven with a big pizza, which we ate at the dining-room table. I thought of the hundreds of meals I'd had at that table, of Chester, of Jerry. And to Gregory it was like a hotel. "Ironically," he said, "my parents set off today to see the Schneiders, and won't be there tonight after all."

I was picking at my pizza, pushing the mushrooms to one side. "Your father didn't seem so bad," I said tentatively.

"Well, he doesn't go around frothing at the mouth," Gregory snapped. "To strangers like you he's perfectly charming. He's one of those people who should only interact with strangers."

"Did they— What did they say about me?"

"They loved you. They want me to marry you." He grinned. "No, they were just amazed—a pretty, nice, normal-seeming girl deigning to go out with me. They couldn't believe it. They thought you must have some hidden motive."

"Did they really *say* that?"

"I can read their thoughts."

"I thought your mother liked you."

"Yes, but she doesn't think anyone could ever like *her* either. She sees us as linked; two impossible people, born to suffer."

I don't know why, but I laughed. Perhaps because he was in a good mood, so did Gregory. "I had a terrific swim," he said. "*You* should swim, Isabel. I could get you into the club."

"I'm a terrible swimmer," I said. "I can't open my eyes under water. I can't breathe through my nose."

"I'll teach you," he said tenderly. "I think you need more physical exercise."

103

I hate it when people tell me what I need. "I'm fine," I snapped. "Please don't criticize me."

Gregory looked horrified. "I'm not! Criticize you? How could I? It's not . . . You have a beautiful body." He blushed. "It's not that, I just thought . . ." He got up and hugged me from behind. "I'm so lucky," he said.

Olive's bed had soft green sheets with wavy lines. Somehow, to our surprise, everything was fine. We did it, and just at the end, as we were lying there, still enveloped in each other's bodies, Gregory said, "This is amazing."

"Better than swimming?"

"Better than anything. . . . Here I was, ten time *more* nervous this time than I was in Princeton, but somehow . . . I don't know."

We both laughed. "I guess we both have a knack for it."

"I love this room," he said enthusiastically. "This is a wonderful apartment: the colors, the prints. It's so artistic. I wouldn't think Stuart would have this kind of apartment."

"Why not?"

"He doesn't seem that aware somehow," Gregory said. "He seems like someone who goes through life unthinkingly."

"No," I said. "He doesn't."

"He and Ketti Anderson are a perfect combination. I don't think they know what emotion is. Maybe they'll never experience the depths of despair, but they'll never know the heights, they'll never experience what we're experiencing right now."

Why, oh why were we talking about Stuart? I sighed and kissed Gregory. "I'm getting so sleepy," I said.

"Just go to sleep," he whispered. "I'll clear up inside."

I lay in bed, hearing Gregory rummage around in the kitchen. I felt good, relieved that Gregory had come. I was amazed at the ease with which our bodies seemed to know what to do. It was nearly midnight. Stuart and Ketti right now are . . . No, they're at some party, flirting with other people. They're miserable, having fucked up on their interviews. I drifted off to sleep.

In the morning we did it again. "I can't believe this,"

Gregory said. "I wonder if I'll start writing badly now. I've never been happy before." He looked a little worried.

"Happiness never lasts," I said to reassure him.

At that he looked agonized. "What do you mean? That you don't care for me anymore?"

"No, of course not . . . I was just thinking of the long run."

"You mean that we'll break up? That we'll tire of each other?"

"Not even that—just that maybe one gets used to being happy and takes it for granted."

"Never," he asserted vehemently. "I've been miserable so long, you can depend on one thing: I'll *never* take it for granted. It's such a pity I'm an atheist. I wish I could offer prayers to some deity or other."

I went in to make breakfast. There was a mix for blueberry muffins, and Gregory said he liked eggs, so I thought I'd scramble some. Pretty soon the coffee was humming along. Gregory came in, freshly showered and dressed. I was in one of Olive's robes, a lovely violet silk with big capelike sleeves. I felt like a courtesan, especially when I thought of my terry-cloth robe at home, which was unraveling at the edges. Olive had the Sunday paper delivered, and we were still sitting around at noon, having more coffee and reading, when the door opened. It was Stuart. He stared. "I must have the wrong apartment," he said.

I blushed. "Where's Ketti?" I asked stupidly.

"At home. Where *should* she be?" He looked at Gregory, who was calmly and proprietarily eating one of my muffins. "What are *you* doing here?"

"I'm here with Isabel," Gregory said. He seemed totally unperturbed.

"Olive said it was okay," I stammered. "She said we could stay here. She and Jerry are in Washington."

"I *know* they're in Washington," Stuart snapped. He came over to me and lifted up one of the sleeves of her robe. "You're wearing her robe. Did she say you could do that too?"

"I didn't think she'd mind." Why was I acting so guilty

and mouselike? "We have a perfect right to be here," I said, trying to stare him down. "You weren't expected back until evening."

"Says who? I'm back now."

"Want some breakfast?" I tried smiling. "The muffins are still warm."

He looked at them with distaste. "They're burned. Anyway, I ate already."

Gregory was reading the book review. "They taste delicious," he said. "Especially with honey."

Stuart looked around the kitchen. "What a mess! Look at this! Eggshells on the counter, the milk's out." He began putting everything back.

"I was going to clean up," I said.

Suddenly I felt miserable, rotten, an impostor. Before Stuart's arrival I felt gay and lighthearted, enjoying Gregory's happiness and the familiarity of being in Olive's apartment with the unfamiliarity of the circumstances. Now it all seemed false. Meretricious. What was I doing in Olive's violet robe, staining the sleeves with muffin batter? What was I doing leading Gregory on, pretending to be in love with him? No, I'd never said specifically "I love you," but everyone knows you can lead someone on with actions as well as words. I felt Stuart could see through the whole situation— must realize, with total contempt, that I had staged it all for his benefit, and that it was a pathetic sham.

Gregory, who was leafing calmly and contentedly through the book review, suddenly looked awkward, ungainly, with his huge hands and strange, yellowish fingernails. He was acting as though Stuart were the impostor, which in one sense he was, and maybe he was enjoying playing lord of the manor in his own way—which also made me sick with self-consciousness. My loyalties now belonged to Gregory, but a tiny, perverse side of me was linked with Stuart.

"Don't you love this quote, Isabel? Listen," Gregory said, as if Stuart, who was still cleaning up in the kitchen, weren't there. "It's from Max Beerbohm. He says, 'True happiness is dining with old friends, writing something that you care
106

about, or traveling south with someone your conscience permits you to love.' Isn't that wonderful?''

It was a good quote, but my ability to react to it, even to take it in, was severely diminished by Stuart's presence. ''It's really witty,'' I said despondently.

''Who's Max Beerbohm?'' Stuart asked, his back still turned.

''Oh, a turn-of-the-century essayist,'' Gregory said. ''Didn't we study him in English? Perhaps not. He's one of Tate O'Reilly's favorites.''

I hated his calling Mr. O'Reilly Tate, and I hated Stuart for his tiny, unerring jabs, designed to bring out just what he knew I would dislike most in Gregory—his pretentiousness. ''Aren't you done?'' I said suddenly, sharply, to Stuart.

He looked at me with a deceptively bland expression. ''I thought I'd fix myself a little lunch,'' he said. ''I had breakfast five hours ago. . . . Unless it would interfere in some way—''

I was about to say it would, but Gregory said, ''No, go right ahead.'' He was still buried in the book review. I picked up the arts and leisure section, because it was on top of the pile. I didn't really care which movies had opened, but I pretended to be engrossed as Stuart fixed his lunch. ''Where are the eggs?'' he asked.

''I scrambled them all,'' I muttered.

''All? Every last one?''

I didn't reply.

''Well, thank God there are a few hard-boiled ones.'' Stuart proceeded to compose his favorite sandwich—several hard-boiled eggs squashed between pumpernickel bread spread with mayonnaise and mustard, with salt and pepper and leaves of lettuce. He took a big bite. ''This is great,'' he said cheerfully. Then he looked up. ''Where's the arts and leisure section?''

I glared at him. ''I'm reading it.''

''Are you almost done?''

''No, I've just started.'' In fact, all I'd been doing was staring at the front page for five minutes.

''I guess I should have gotten my own paper . . . though

107

I thought this *was* my own paper, in that it was delivered to *my* apartment.''

I flung the arts and leisure section at him. ''Oh take it, for Christ's sake!'' I went inside to shower. Usually on Sunday morning I washed my hair and then sat quietly and let it dry. I loved that ritual. I wanted to leave both of them and go home and wash my hair. Instead, I showered in Olive's bathroom, used her shampoo, and got dressed.

When I returned to the kitchen, Gregory was reading the arts and leisure section and Stuart was reading the book review. They both looked up at me. ''The shower's free,'' I said, ''in case anyone wants to use it.''

''I have my own shower,'' Stuart said, ''and my own bathroom, even.''

''Would your friend mind?'' Gregory asked. ''Olive?''

''She's not *her* friend,'' Stuart said. ''She's *my* mother.''

''She wouldn't mind,'' I said, ignoring him.

Gregory got up and stretched. ''That was a wonderful breakfast, Isabel. The best I've ever had.''

''Thanks,'' I said, and blushed since, somehow, under the circumstances, that seemed a veiled sexual allusion.

When Gregory left the room, Stuart looked at me and smiled in our old complicitous, mocking way.

I cleared my throat. ''Look,'' I said, ''I don't want one fucking word out of you. Do you get that? Not one. We were here, we were having a lovely time, Olive said we could stay here. . . . You come barging in—''

''Barging?'' Stuart looked amazed. ''Into my own apartment? It's past noon, it's Sunday. Am I supposed to sit in the lobby for five hours, while you and—''

''Stuart, I mean it. Gregory is my guest, and I don't want to hear anything you have to say about him.'' I primly sipped at my cold coffee.

He burst out laughing. ''Your *guest*? Is that the word? Sorry, I'm just not up on the intricacies of these things.''

''I'm not going to talk anymore,'' I announced. ''You can talk, I'm just not going to reply.''

''Great,'' Stuart said. ''I love a good listener.'' But he shut up too. We sat in dogged silence reading, or pretending to read, the Sunday *Times*, until Gregory emerged, fresh-faced and clean, with a big grin on his face.

"What a wonderful shower!" he said. "I feel terrific." Then he looked at Stuart.

Stuart looked up. "I think I'll take a walk," he said. "See you later."

We didn't say anything as he got into his boots and winter coat.

It looked rotten out to me—half snow, half rain, one of those days when it gets dark so early in the afternoon that the daylight hours seem minuscule. After Stuart left, Gregory sat down and said, "I feel horribly guilty."

"Why should you?"

"Well, it *is* his apartment. We made him feel unwanted."

"He *was* unwanted," I cried. "What right did he have to return at noon?"

"But he didn't know."

"He could have walked right out again." I pouted. "He spoiled everything. We were having such a nice breakfast, it was quiet and intimate, and now it's all ruined."

Gregory squeezed my hands. "No, it's not. Not at all. We had a wonderful evening, and well, he's on a walk now—" He looked at me hopefully.

I gathered that meant did I want to pop back into bed and take advantage of Stuart's temporary absence. I didn't. I felt as unsexy as one could possibly feel, and I was certain, even if we did it at record speed, Stuart would manage to walk in right as one of us was about to come. "Maybe we should both go home," I said tentatively. "Would that be okay?"

"Oh, of course, I was being extremely insensitive. Anyway, he might come back, the weather looks so rotten. And your parents must be expecting you."

Oh yes, my parents—I hadn't given a thought to them in the past twenty-four hours.

Gregory left first, and I tidied up a bit, though in truth Stuart had done an amazingly good job with the kitchen. There was nothing left to do, really, but stack the Sunday *Times* in a neat pile. I left a note on Olive's pillow saying,

"Thanks!" That seemed inadequate, but it was all I was up to.

Strangely, my parents weren't home. Not that they never went out, but I had been sure that on this particular weekend they would be sitting there, listening to every creak in the hall. There was no note—but why should there be, if they were just out at a concert or an art show, or visiting friends? Not that I'd wanted them home. It was a huge relief to be spared having to invent some story about the weekend. At the same time the silence in the apartment seemed ominous. I even looked in their bedroom, which I never do.

I felt violently sleepy, yet it seemed to me I had slept well, and long. I didn't want to fall asleep. I wanted to stay up and catch up on my homework. I brought my papers into the living room and sat down in the armchair, trying to work. A half hour later there was a knock on our door. Somewhat cautiously I asked who it was. "Chester," came the reply.

I opened the door. "Oh, hi," I said weakly. "What's up?"

"I was up at the apartment with some flowers for Olive's birthday. The door was open but nobody was around. I was a little worried."

"She's in Washington with Jerry," I explained. "Stuart's there, but he went for a walk."

"Oh." Chester looked greatly relieved, instead of crushed, as I'd thought he'd be at Olive's being with Jerry. "Well . . . How are things going?"

"She says he's just temporary," I said to cheer him up.

He shrugged sadly. "It's been so long."

"Well, you broke her heart," I said, suddenly annoyed with him and with the male sex in general. "What do you expect?"

"But it was nothing," he said. "It was—" And he began the same long defense of his behavior I'd heard many times.

Maybe it was just my present mood, but I was less patient than usual. "Men never take responsibility for their actions," I said. "They do this, they do that, and they expect women to forgive and forget, to accept anything. It's not fair."

Now Chester looked crushed. "You're right. . . . I was

110

an asshole, a fool. . . . I'm not worthy of her. She would have realized that eventually. But I can give her flowers, can't I?''

"Sure," I said, relenting. "She'll love them. They're beautiful.''

After Chester left, I dozed off in that fitful way where you keep jerking awake and having weird snatches of dreams—anonymous people running up stairs, monsters, car chases. When I heard the key in the front door, I kept my eyes closed. They seemed stuck together. "Hi," I said, waving at what I assumed were my parents. "I'm back."

It was Stuart. He looked annoyed. "So I see."

"Have a nice walk?" I asked sarcastically.

He didn't bother replying. "Someone left a pot of flowers in the hall.''

I yawned. "It was Chester. For Olive's birthday. He came by awhile ago and was worried that the door was open but no one was around. I guess he thought there might have been a break-in.''

Stuart smirked. "There was, I gather.''

"Stuart, please shut up and go home.''

"I'm locked out. El Jerko must have locked it. You have a key, right?''

"Yeah.''

"Look, can I just sit here? I won't even speak. I just— I'm beat.'' Suddenly he did look completely exhausted.

I felt touched. "How was your Harvard interview? I forgot to ask.''

"Lousy. I was nervous, I'm not sure why. I don't have a ghost of a chance anyway. Ketti got a youngish male, who was ready to marry her by the end of hers, so I gather she's a shoo-in, except she doesn't even want to go there.''

"There're other places," I said consolingly.

"True." He just sat, staring at the rug.

"I'm sorry you had to take a walk.''

He smiled wryly. "Listen, could I take a nap in your room? I'm about to crash.''

"Sure. Maybe I will too.''

It was funny what magical powers the nap had, even when

111

we'd been at each other's throats an hour before. We went into my room and lay down in our usual way, back to back, and in moments I was in the best, most contented, secure kind of sleep—the kind you have in childhood.

BLOOMING

Olive was lovely about the weekend. She didn't question me in any way, just said she hoped everything had been fine. She was pleased to find the kitchen so scrupulously clean. "Stuart's always going at me about not putting things away," she said. "He'd murder me if we were married."

I could easily have told her it was Stuart who had cleaned up. I could have told her how I felt about Gregory, about my fluctuating moods. . . . The nice thing about Olive was she was ready to listen to anything, but ready not to listen if you weren't prepared for confidences. My mother, for some reason, kept questioning me. "Pete said he saw you over the weekend," she said. "I thought you were at Lois's."

"I was. He must have meant on Sunday. I came home earlier than I expected."

"I'd swear he said it was Saturday."

"Well, what difference does it make?" I said irritably.

"None at all. I was just asking. . . . Are you getting your period? You seem on edge."

"Mom, I'm *not* on edge, and I'm *not* getting my period. Please stop asking all the time. If you want, I'll

113

give you a calendar with all my period dates marked out so you can know exactly when I get it. Would that make you happy? It just has no bearing whatsoever on my moods.''

My mother looked miffed. "You're lucky, then. At your age I had excruciating cramps. I almost passed out on the street once."

"I'm sorry about that."

"After I went on the pill and then had you, I was fine. Having children cleared it all up—it was like a wonder drug."

"I'm not having children," I said sadistically. I knew, from overheard conversations, how much she was looking forward to being a grandmother, and naturally I was her only avenue to that role.

"Everyone says that at your age," she said, unperturbed.

"Everyone?"

"All intellectual girls. I did. I thought all children were nasty little drooling brats. I hated looking after my younger sister. . . . And then you meet someone, you fall in love, and you want them. It's as simple as that."

It sounded horribly reductive. "But not everyone *does* have them, so there must be some exceptions."

My mother was half reading her cookbook while she spoke to me. "Oh, some women have terrible problems. That's another story. Look at your aunt Rae. She had four miscarriages."

It seemed to me no one could get me as enraged as my mother, though Stuart came a pretty close second. "I meant," I said, speaking very slowly, as though to a hearing-impaired person, "that there are women who don't want them, and who never even try to have them. . . . Katherine Mansfield, Virginia Woolf, Isak Dinesen, Emily Dickinson."

My mother looked at me indulgently. "Oh, darling, that was long ago. Virginia Woolf had all her mental problems, and didn't Dinesen have syphilis from that dreadful man she married in Africa? And Katherine Mansfield died of tuberculosis at thirty-four. They're hardly typical. . . . *You're* not going to be like that."

"How do you know? Anyway, I may just prefer another kind of life. I may not even marry." I felt my mother was getting the upper hand, and that I was sounding increasingly petty and absurd.

"Everyone marries," my mother said. I hated the way she kept reading her recipe while she talked to me.

"Does everyone do *everything*?" I said. "Aren't there *any* individual differences?"

"We're all such creatures of hormonal urges," she said, turning a page. "It's a pity, perhaps. . . . But no, why marry? If you don't want to, don't. Don't just marry for the sake of it, not that your generation *is* doing that. Do exactly as you like."

"That's what I intend to do." I said stiffly. It was peculiar, hearing my mother mention being at the mercy of hormonal urges. Was that what had swept her and my father into each other's arms so many years ago? The idea struck me as absurd—but I couldn't think of any other rational excuses for it.

Olive had asked me to go shopping with her. I loved doing that. She always asked my opinion, even when I was nine or ten. "Are these too gaudy?" she would ask about a lovely pair of red sandals. "Be honest." I never thought they were too gaudy. On her they looked right, elegant, unusual. This time she needed underpants. "They say," Olive said, "you can judge a woman by the color underpants she chooses. White is virginal and black is sexy—I forget what the others are. I must be schizophrenic, because I like all colors." She was looking at the lace-trimmed bikinis on the rack.

I decided I must be at the bottom of the barrel, because I still wore plain cotton underpants and picked bras that were easy to take off. But I stood beside her, looking wistfully at the bikini styles as though I were a member of some third sex that could never wear them.

"What's interesting," Olive said, "is they claim women

115

buy their underwear for men, whereas I've never met a man who cared one way or the other. They just want to see you without anything on at all."

When I was with Olive, I always felt a touch of my mother creep into me; it wasn't disapproval, just the awareness that even now it made me uncomfortable to talk about these topics. I supposed I must be a sex object to Gregory, but I certainly didn't feel like one, even while I was with him.

Olive ended up getting some men's-style women's underpants, like boxer shorts. "Just for a change," she said. "Jerry hates them, and I'm getting ready to boot him. That's how I know I'm about to boot someone—I start doing everything they hate. It's so silly, really. Why not just be open about it?" She handed the saleswoman her credit card.

"I've never booted anyone," I mused. "I've never had anyone to boot."

"Well, you're still young," Olive said sweetly, though I knew she had booted several by the time she was my age.

We went for coffee afterward. "This is why I always wanted a daughter," she said, "all these things you could never do with a son."

Of course, I never did them with my mother. "I like it too," I said shyly.

Olive was pouring her usual two packs of sugar into her cappuccino. "Isabel"—she leaned forward—"I want to ask you something. Do you think Stuart is in some kind of funk?"

"What kind of funk?"

"Oh, he just seems so touchy lately, so crabby, picking on me. . . . Of course, he's still a teenager, but when he was younger he was so mature and calm. Now he really gets me furious at times. Maybe *I'm* just getting touchier. He criticizes Jerry, he criticizes Chester. He said that lovely bunch of flowers Chester sent me for my birthday was funereal. It wasn't."

"I know," I said, drinking my bitter espresso. "I thought

it was lovely too," and I told her how Chester had come over, because he thought there had been a break-in.

"Oh, that weekend you—"

I blushed and ducked my head. I doubted Stuart had told her about his returning at noon, but it was still embarrassing.

"Maybe," Olive mused, "it's that he sees you happy, in love, *and* with a suitable person. I'm not saying you'll marry him, but Gregory sounds like a perfect darling. Your father was telling me what wonderful poetry he writes. . . . And here's Stuart, stuck with that Ketti creature, and who is he fooling, really?"

I wanted to tell her she had it all wrong, but I couldn't. "She's beautiful," I said. "And I think he knows it's temporary. I think that's what he wants."

"Oh, of course!" Olive agreed. "Everything is temporary at your age, and should be. But why isn't she making him happy? *You* look happy."

"I do?"

"Yes, you look radiant, really blooming. Your hair, your skin . . ."

"Maybe men don't do that," I offered. "Bloom, I mean."

She sighed. "I don't know. Of course he's my son, so I probably have no perspective at all. If I were married, I could discuss it with my partner. But Jerry doesn't care about kids. That's why he didn't have them. *He* wants to be the permanent child."

I thought of the conversation with my mother. "Are you sorry you had children?" I said. "I don't mean Stuart in particular, but just at all? You could have led a much freer life, otherwise."

Olive looked surprised. "I really couldn't have. I've been as free as my personality has let me be. No, I wish, if anything, I'd had more. I wish I'd had one with Chester."

I smiled wryly. "He would have loved it. . . . He still would."

"Yes, but he was so young . . . and then, if we'd broken up, he would have wanted joint custody. With Marcel it was simple. He just writes Stuart once a year, and at twenty-one

117

he'll send for him and give him a man-to-man talk. What I wonder is whether Stuart has had enough male companionship. Chester was more like an older brother, Jerry ignores him. . . ."

"I think Stuart's okay," I said tentatively. "It's been good for me—almost like having a brother."

She looked delighted. "That's how he feels too. You've been *such* a good influence. I think real brothers and sisters tend to fight like cats and dogs, or to back off when there's any hint of sexual closeness, as there often is in adolescence. I know there was with *my* brother. But you can have the best of both worlds."

I thought of our naps, our lying chastely and comfortably back to back, and how now there was beginning to seem something peculiar about it. What would Stuart do if, instead of turning so my behind touched his, I flung my leg over his and kissed him on the lips? "What will you do," I asked, to banish these thoughts, "after pitching Jerry?"

She frowned. "What *should* I do? What do *you* think?"

It was the way she asked me, when I was nine, for my opinion on shoes. Me! An expert on men! "Is there anyone else—"

"No one I can't live without."

"There's always Chester."

"No," Olive said firmly. "There really isn't. Not in the sense you mean. I love Chester, and I wish him the best. I hope we'll always stay in touch, but things *do* end, you know. It's pathetic and demeaning to deny that."

I don't know why, until that moment, I hadn't thought of that in relation to Stuart and myself. We were going off, in a matter of months, to different colleges. Our relationship was probably based entirely on proximity, on the fact that we had keys to each other's apartments. It created a kind of closeness that I didn't have even with Lois. I thought of how it would be the following year, when we came home on vacations—stiff conversations in the hall, "How's it going?"

Olive was watching me intently, and I had the feeling she

118

interpreted my stricken expression as having something to do with Gregory. "It's not," she said, "that I think absence in itself is a bad thing. It can be a really good thing. I just meant some relationships change, and they can't change back."

We can always exchange letters, I thought to console myself.

SHELTERED LIVES

It was in March—before we found out about which colleges we'd gotten into, before the weather had turned really warm and springlike—that Andria found a lump in her breast. She had a biopsy and was told she needed surgery. It happened quickly, over spring vacation, and she was in the hospital and operated on two days later.

The four of us hadn't done as many things together this year as we had in years past. Maybe it was the pairing off into couples: Hal and Andria, Stuart and Ketti, me and Gregory, Lois and no one. So when we met in Andria's room at the hospital, we felt funny together, not as at ease as we might have been a year earlier. Andria was by far the healthiest of the four of us. It seemed particularly strange to see her lying there in a hospital bed, looking weak and pale.

We sat around her bed self-consciously, Lois biting her cuticles since her nails were bitten down to the quick, Ketti fiddling with her hair and asking a lot of brisk, technical questions about breast cancer and lumpectomies, but not looking at Andria.

"It's not uncommon," Andria said. "Look, the tumor

120

was small and was caught in its early stages. I'm young, I still have my breasts. Don't worry about me. Really. I'm going to be okay. It's Hal I'm worried about. He's a nervous wreck. Have you seen him?''

We hadn't. "Take care of him, will you?" she said, as though he were a child. "Reassure him. I'm not going to die, for heaven's sake."

Lois and I exchanged glances. If it had been either of us in that hospital bed, we would have been writing our obituaries.

"Are we tiring you?" Ketti asked. We'd already been in her room a half hour.

"Maybe just a little. But it is so great to see you. And I'll be home in a day or so." She hugged us all, one by one.

We trooped out silently and there, in the hall, was Hal, looking forlorn and pathetic. "How is she?" he said, or rather whispered. "Is she tired?"

"A bit," Ketti said, taking him by the arm. "Come and have coffee with us. Then you can come back later."

We found a coffee shop nearby with a large booth. Hal sat next to Ketti, I sat across with Lois. He just stared blankly into space. Ketti squeezed his shoulder. "She's okay. She's going to be fine," she said.

"But it's so unfair," Hal said in a high shrill voice. "She's always been so healthy! And she's such a good, kind person. Why should anything bad happen to *her*?" He looked at us almost accusingly, as though wondering why it hadn't happened to any of us instead.

"Life is unfair," Lois said bleakly.

"Andria's going to be fine," Ketti said again, patting him, hugging him. "I know it, Hal. . . . You'll get married and have a wonderful family. This is just—temporary. And it'll make you savor life all the more, savor what you have."

"I do savor it," he said bitterly. On the one hand we were impressed by his sorrow and despair. It was so clear he saw his whole life connected to Andria, their fates linked. But he also seemed extremely young to us, almost petulant, as though his grief were as much for himself as for Andria. We

121

were torn between feeling this was "the real thing" and wanting to tell him to shape up.

I walked home with Lois, slowly. We held hands, the way we used to do when we were children, for comfort. We didn't speak, but it was the comfortable silence of two people who each knew what the other was thinking. Perhaps it was in contrast to this wordless rapport that first Gregory, then Stuart, seemed so intolerable.

Gregory was sick. At first they'd thought he had pneumonia, but it turned out to be bronchitis. He'd lost his voice and regained it, but still had a hacking cough. I hadn't seen him since the illness began, because he was supposedly contagious. "The doctor says you can come over Saturday," he said excitedly. "I can't wait."

"Don't you want to know how Andria was?"

"Oh right, how was she?" But he sounded like he was just being cued to ask the right question.

"Well, she looks pale, but she's in good spirits. It's Hal who's a wreck."

"Yeah, I can imagine. . . . Well, listen, what time Saturday would be good for you? Do you want to come for lunch? Or later in the afternoon?"

"I don't know if I want to come at all," I snapped.

There was a stunned silence. "Why? What's wrong? What happened?"

"One of my best friends is in the hospital. She could die . . . and all you care about is when I can visit you!"

"No," Gregory protested. "That's *not* it. It's just . . . I've been looking forward to seeing you so much. And I hardly know Andria."

"Men are just terminally insensitive," I cried. "Is it genetic, or what?" I knew this would wound Gregory, who considered himself unusually sensitive and a feminist.

"Please come," he begged. "I'm sorry if I gave the wrong reaction. I wasn't thinking."

"I'll call you Saturday," I said, and slammed down the phone.

All he could think of was seeing me and having sex. Andria was nothing to him, just a girl from school he hardly

122

knew. I felt tense and roiled up and tried taking a walk, but it was so windy my eyes teared, and I finally came home.

I met Stuart coming up in the elevator carrying two bags of groceries. Without asking, he just handed me one. "Do I get a tip?" I asked sarcastically.

"These are damn heavy," he said. "Just help me get them into the kitchen."

When we'd put down the grocery bags, I told him about my fight with Gregory. I expected Stuart would take my side. Instead he said, "Give the guy a break, Iz. You're his girl-friend, he hasn't seen you in a week. It seems like years to him." He grinned. "Maybe he's getting a little horny." He opened a can of apple juice and started drinking it.

"You're really repulsive," I said, wanting to hit him. "I don't know how you can live with yourself."

"Do I have a choice? Look, I happen to know exactly what Gregory is feeling. It's that the minute anything happens to one of the four of you, it's full-scale female bonding. You're all there, gathered together, giving each other support, warmth. Where do *we* come in? We're these irrelevant beings who fuck you occasionally, *if* you deign. But what if I'd been run over and you walked past? Would you give a damn? Would you even call an ambulance?"

"No! I certainly wouldn't. I'd leave you there to die an agonizing death, which you'd deserve." And I slammed out of his apartment.

I called Lois and asked if I could come for dinner. I wanted to be with someone who cared about Andria.

She sounded surprised. "Sure. . . . You sound funny. Are you okay?"

"I'll explain later."

We didn't talk a lot at dinner about Andria, but Miller was very nice, totally different from Gregory or Stuart.

He leaned over and patted my hand. "Don't be sad, Isa-bel. Andria will be fine. But I know what a shock it is."

Suddenly I burst out telling how Gregory had acted. "Why are men *like* that?" I asked Miller. I thought maybe since he was one, but a better, more mature version, he could give some clue.

"Oh, I think at times like this people retreat. They don't know what to say. When Lois's mother was so ill, some people would literally cross the street when they saw me coming, or just babble on about some insane trivia, never mentioning Ginger at all. Anything but discussing the truth. It terrified them. Emotion *terrifies* people."

"Not just men or boys?"

"Maybe more so in that they've had very little experience in dealing with it, but no, I don't see it as sex related. When Ginger was dying, certain men were wonderful. Just by calling, or writing a note. Your father, for instance."

I was startled. My father? He seemed the last person on earth capable of dealing with emotion of any kind.

"Each week he would call, or send me a note or some little gift, like a quote he thought might be helpful. I treasure those. At times like that, you see through to the real person beneath and, once having seen it, you never forget."

That was all amazing to me. I was fond of my father, and at heart had often sided with him when my mother went at him. But he seemed to live in some world beyond the one Miller was referring to, the tender, responsive one.

Later Lois and I lay in bed and talked. "I was thinking," Lois said, "how sad I would be if it had been you in that hospital bed."

I hadn't thought that about Lois, and I felt guilty. "Would you have carried on like Hal?" I asked.

"Yes," Lois said. "I probably would have—but in a subtler way."

"I certainly hope so," I said. "He really sounded as if he thought his world was coming to a crashing end. Though I did feel sorry for him. He seemed sincere."

"Yes," Lois said. She reached over and squeezed my hand. "I'm sorry Gregory was so awful . . . and then Stuart too."

124

"I *don't* think our caring is female bonding," I said, indignant all over again. "It's *friendship*."

"I guess with Gregory maybe it's jealousy. He wants to think you're only concerned about him."

I looked up at Lois's ceiling. "I feel like such a sham most of the time," I said. "I'm not even in love with him."

"Do you tell him you are?"

"No, but I think he assumes I'm the kind of girl who wouldn't go to bed with someone unless she *was* in love with him."

"Everyone probably assumes that about you," Lois said. "I did. Whereas, really, you just wanted to see what it was like, wasn't that it? To see if it was all it was cracked up to be?"

I still couldn't admit to Lois that one of my motives had been to get Stuart jealous. "I guess," I said weakly.

"And is it?" she pursued relentlessly.

I sighed, feeling trapped. "It's, well . . . I can see how you could get to enjoy it. I *do* enjoy it at times. But I'm not in love with him. So it isn't . . . earthshaking and all that."

Lois heaved a snort of disgust. "That's such sexist bullshit! . . . Maybe men just don't turn you on."

"I don't know," I said. "Maybe I *should* have waited for being in love."

"It *is* kind of pathetic, the way Gregory droops after you at school," Lois said.

I giggled, meanly. "He's writing all these poems about it. One's going to be in the yearbook."

"Isabel! What will you do? How embarrassing!"

"No, it's full of metaphors, and terribly obscure. Anyway, doesn't everyone know?"

"I think people assume you're in love with him, or that you're a couple at any rate."

"Not like Hal and Andria?"

"No, more like Stuart and Ketti."

"I bet they're not in love either."

125

"But no one expects *them* to be. With them it's purely physical."

I thought of my own tentative love poetry, to which Mr. O'Reilly had reacted so scornfully. I was just as glad it would never be seen by anyone except him. If I couldn't even make Lois understand how I felt, I didn't want to try with anyone else.

SPRING

Spring came, real spring. I got into a bunch of colleges, including Swarthmore, where I'd decided to go. Gregory got into Columbia, Stuart into Haverford, Lois into Mount Holyoke, Ketti into Harvard, Andria and Hal into Stanford. Everyone was fairly content, my parents especially because I'd applied to the University of California at Santa Cruz and to Reed, all the way across the country, and decided against them. They knew that hadn't been because I couldn't bear to be so far away from them, but they didn't care.

Olive said I should come over and celebrate, that she'd finally booted Jerry and it could be a twin celebration. I'd seen him moving out, actually, just after I'd opened my Swarthmore acceptance letter. I went out into the hall, wanting to go over and tell Stuart, when Jerry appeared with a suitcase and a few boxes, looking angry. "What do you want?" he said, scowling.

"I got into Swarthmore," I said gaily, in that dumbly jubilant mood where you expect everyone to share your joy.

"So? What difference will that make? If you hadn't gone there, you'd have gone somewhere else. You kids are so damn spoiled. Your whole life is handed to you on a platter. Like Stuart. Thank God I didn't have kids. If I had a brat like that, I'd have knocked some sense into him by now."

For some reason I laughed. Partly it was nervousness. I'd never heard anyone talk like that. Then I remembered he was being booted and probably feeling badly about it. "I'm sorry," I said, suddenly contrite.

He stood there, arms akimbo. "What're you sorry *about*, Isabel?" He drawled my name.

"Just that you . . . that it didn't work out with you and Olive."

"Oh great, she's told *you* all about it too. Maybe it's in *The New York Times*. I better get a copy to check."

He looked menacing, and his mood seemed so ugly that I started back to my own apartment. "Where are you going?" he said.

"No place special."

"Just taking up space in the hall? Well, why don't you give me some help if you're not doing anything?"

After a brief inner debate—he did have three large boxes— I helped him with them into the elevator. "Come on down and help me get them in a cab. That fucking doorman's always asleep when you need him."

We stood silently in the elevator. Jerry was watching me with a scornful expression; my heart was thumping. I wasn't sure if I was being foolish, but I hated giving in to that cowardly side of myself. Suddenly, he leaned over and, putting one hand on each side of me, kissed me on the lips, hard. He smiled at the terrified expression on my face. "Maybe we'll be trapped in the elevator," he said. "Then you'll have something to tell your girlfriends about."

We didn't get stuck in the elevator, and Pete, who was on duty, instantly appeared and began carrying Jerry's boxes out to the street. "So long," Jerry called. "Good luck at Swarthmore."

I didn't really feel I'd been in any danger. I was pretty sure Jerry's macho swagger was a put-on. Nonetheless I felt weak-kneed as I went up in the elevator again.

128

Stuart was in the hall. "Hey, I got into Haverford!" he cried, hugging me and lifting me up in the air.

"I got into Swarthmore!" I showed him the letter.

"Where were you? Your mother said you came over to tell me."

I flushed. "I got roped into helping Jerry move his stuff."

"Why? Let the creep move it himself."

"I should have." I told him about the incident in the elevator. "Nothing would have happened," I said quickly when I saw Stuart's expression. "It was just—"

"That fucker," Stuart said. "What do you mean nothing would have happened? You could be pregnant by now. You could be about to have twins when you start your winter term. What would Swarthmore say about that?"

"I wonder why Olive put up with him for so long."

"Maybe he's great in bed . . . only neither of us will ever know, and I personally think that's no excuse."

"You!" I laughed.

"What does *that* mean?"

"Who are you to talk?"

"Who am I to talk about what?"

"Well, you and Ketti—isn't that just a physical thing?"

"As opposed to what you and Arrington are doing—sitting around discussing Victorian sonnets? God, Iz, you get me so damn mad. When *I* do something, it's this animal act, groveling around in the mud, but if *you* do the exact same thing, it's on some higher level, souls communing." He shook his head in disgust.

He had a point, but I didn't feel like backing down. "I'm not saying it's *all* spiritual with us," I said. "But it's a meeting of minds as well."

"Ketti has a mind, for Christ's sake, a fine mind. . . . Just because her body isn't bad doesn't detract from her mind. Besides, I thought you were saying just the other day how insensitive and cloddish old Gregory was about Andria." He beamed with that "now I've got you" expression.

"He was sick—he wasn't himself," I said. "And you were just as bad and you weren't even sick."

"But we're not having an affair."

129

"Who said we were? What does *that* have to do with it?"

For some reason we both suddenly laughed. "Why are we doing this?" Stuart said. "We should be celebrating. Ol finally booted Jerry, we got into great colleges."

"You're right. . . . No, I *was* feeling good. I was just coming over to say that when I ran into Jerry in the hallway." I shuddered. "I guess he did kind of scare me. I know it's all swagger."

Stuart put his arm around me. "Poor Iz. I wish I'd been there. I could have socked him."

"I can defend myself," I said weakly, not pulling away.

He grinned. "Yeah, I know. One left to the jaw and he would have been spinning. . . . And listen, I take back what I said about Gregory. I don't know him. He has to have virtues if you picked him. You wouldn't pick just anybody."

"Right, and same with Ketti, whom I do know," I said. "I'm just jealous because she's got everything. She's smart and sexy. I've envied her for years. Now she even has you."

That last popped out unexpectedly.

"Well, she deserves better and you do too, and by next year this time you'll both—"

I felt sad, thinking of that. "It's funny, I know I should be feeling good. I do in one way, but it's like everything's breaking up, the 'fearsome foursome,' us . . ."

"*We're* not breaking up," Stuart said gently.

"I mean, in the sense that we've always lived on the same floor, it's been so easy to just drop back and forth. Next year we'll meet on vacations and it'll be horribly stiff and awkward."

"No," he said. "Nothing of the kind. We'll see each other a lot. Haverford's right next to Swarthmore."

"It's still the end of something," I insisted. "Everything seems so fragile somehow. Relationships, life . . ."

Stuart looked away. "Yeah, well . . ."

"It's just a mood," I said quickly.

"Right. . . . See you at dinner then?"

My mother was indignant that the celebration dinner was to be at Olive's. "Then tell Stuart he must come here over the weekend. I'll make all his favorites."

"I will." I glanced at my father, who was immersed in a book, and on impulse went over and kissed him on the forehead.

He looked up with a bemused smile. "What's this?"

"Just thinking that I'll miss you next year." I'd also been thinking of what Miller had said, about how thoughtful my father had been when Lois's mother was sick.

"I'm so glad you won't be going to one of those ghastly places on the West Coast," my father said. He had this image of the West Coast as a place of sun-bronzed fools, chanting mantras and wearing beads.

"I am too." I wanted, somehow, to draw something more out of him. "Lois's father was saying the other day how much he treasured the notes you wrote him when his wife was ill. I didn't know you had."

Surprisingly, my father reddened. "Yes, well . . . people need to feel someone cares at a time like that."

Drawing my father out was harder than pulling a tooth. I'm sure he felt he shared a lot with me, just by taking me on his photography expeditions. The rest was locked inside.

Olive and Stuart had prepared a joint meal. I was surprised to see Chester there too, stirring something wonderful-smelling in a large pot. "This will be a meal to remember," he said, "a vegetable curry not to be surpassed."

Had Chester been reinstated? So quickly? It didn't seem to square with what Olive had said. As though sensing my confusion, Olive drew me aside. "Chester is family," she said. "I had to call him to tell him about Stuart's getting into Haverford."

"I like Chester," I said. "I always did." I hadn't told Olive about the Jerry incident in the elevator, and I hoped Stuart hadn't. There didn't seem any point. He was gone, finis, not someone who would be around years hence, transformed from lover to friend with no hard feelings.

Chester had brought champagne and we were all in a celebratory mood. Olive had piled her hair up, but it began falling down in tendrils. "I want to drink to all of you," she said. "My family. I want you to know I love you all."

"We love you too," Chester said, moist-eyed.

"In a way this is an ending with Isabel and Stuart going off to college," she said, "but it's not really. Every ending is also a beginning."

"Hear, hear," Stuart said.

As we sat down to eat, Stuart's father (whom Olive had called earlier to tell about Stuart's getting into college) called from France, wanting to speak to Stuart. He excused himself and went into the other room.

"I thought Marcel ought to know," Olive said, though neither Chester nor I had questioned it. "He *is* his father, after all."

"A very bad father, " Chester said severely.

"You mean in not being around?" Olive said.

"He plants a seed, then vanishes. . . . What kind of father is that?" Chester wanted to know.

"Some men are just like that," Olive said. "Maybe they lack the gene for sticking around, for monogamy, for wanting to get involved in parenthood in that nitty-gritty way. What do you think, Isabel?"

As always, I was flattered at her asking me. "*My* father's stuck around," I said.

Chester looked irritated. "I hate these generalizations. My father was *not* like that. He loved us, he was involved. I, if I am ever a father, will be involved. You picked a dud," he said accusingly. "You've coped very well on your own, but that's no excuse for *him*."

"Well, it's all so long ago," Olive said vaguely. "He was gorgeous then, and I've always had a weakness for handsome men."

Chester blushed, since this presumably included him. "You are beautiful," he said, gazing at her adoringly.

Impulsively Olive reached over and squeezed Chester's hand.

Chester looked surprised at this gesture. I wondered how much of it to attribute to the champagne, how much to the sentiment of the occasion. Just then Stuart came back. "Well, I've got the old man's blessing," he said. "Not that he knows Haverford from a hole in the wall. But he's very pleased. He knew I had it in me. He wants me to come to France this summer—he'll pay. I'll fly to Paris and take the train down to Marseilles.''

"How generous," said Olive, a bit ironically.

"Oh, and listen to this," Stuart said. "I love this. We're going through all this man-to-man shit and at the end he says, 'One word of advice: Avoid the prostitutes in Paris.' '' He roared with laughter. "As though that was the first thing I was going to do when I got there.''

"He's living in another century," Olive said, looking disgusted. "Are you really going to go?''

"Sure, why not? He has lots of little, how did he put it, hot-eyed Mediterranean beauties for me to sample. It sounds like an hors d'oeuvre at a Greek restaurant.''

"How about Ketti?" Chester asked.

Stuart reached for the yogurt-and-cucumber dish. "Oh, we'll be a thing of the past by then.''

"It wasn't true love?" Chester said, seeming disappointed.

Stuart shrugged. "I'm just a kid—give me time.''

"I was in love for the first time at fourteen," Chester said. "True love . . . You're not too young.''

"I'm immature," Stuart said. "Ask Iz.''

They all looked at me. I felt embarrassed. "Well . . .''

"She doesn't like to rail at me when other people are around," Stuart said. "She has too kind a heart.''

Chester raised his glass. "To Isabel's kind heart.''

After we'd clinked glasses, toasts were proposed to Olive's having pitched Jerry, to Chester's curry, to Stuart's and my brilliant educational opportunities. After dinner Chester and Olive disappeared, while Stuart and I did the dishes. I looked inquiringly in the direction of Olive's bedroom.

"Search me," Stuart said. "Stranger things have happened.''

"I like Chester," I said, putting a rinsed plate in the dishwasher.

Stuart hugged me. "That's because of your kind heart," he said.

With a guilty pang I thought of Gregory, of Lois, of my parents. "Not a very consistent one."

Stuart thought I meant him. "Oh, I deserve it most of the time. And even with me, you're not that bad. You try and keep me in shape."

"Oh, it's not just you," I said. "Even with Gregory, I'm just using him. It's so cold-blooded and cynical. He's writing these sonnets about me, he's been sick, and I never think of him. Hardly ever, anyway."

"Iz, come on. You've made the guy's year. You've changed his whole self-image. A blind person can see it. . . . He's stunned that you went for him. It's the most flattering thing that'll ever happen to him, I bet."

I sighed. "It's sweet, your trying to find excuses, but . . . I'm terrible with my mother, I bark at her—"

"Everyone barks at their mother," Stuart said. "I bark at Olive all the time."

I was sinking into what seemed a bottomless vat of self-pity and remorse. "I'm just a bad person," I said. "I seem to everyone to be what I'm not. I'm deceitful, I tell lies, I have mixed emotions about just about anything you can name, I—"

With mock sternness Stuart said, "Well, I'm glad I know. If I'd known all this earlier, I would never have allowed you to be my friend. I'm shocked, horrified."

I giggled. "It's worse than you think. You think I tell you everything. I don't. There are things I'm not telling you right now when I'm pretending to be telling you everything."

"So? I don't tell you everything either—should we take each other to court?" He came closer. "You know what you need?" I thought he was going to say a sock in the jaw, but he said, "A good back rub, that's the thing. I learned how from Ketti. It eases out all this garbage."

This made me anxious. "Do I have to take my clothes off?"

Stuart grinned. "Not unless you have a compelling need to." He took my hand and led me out to the living room. "No, look, it's simple. You just lie down on the couch and

I'll rub your back. There are certain pressure points that knot up, and if you ease them out, it'll do you a world of good.''

Stuart knelt beside me and began massaging my back. "Does that feel better?" he said.

"Yeah, definitely, great." I sat up. "I'm sorry I can't do the same to you. I don't know how."

"Someday I'll show you." We looked at each other, having come too close to conceal everything but still holding back.

I stood up. "Thank Olive for the lovely dinner," I said, suddenly formal.

"I will, if she ever comes out of her room."

At home I thought of Olive with such intense envy it was like a sharp pain in my side. She had pitched Jerry, she didn't want Chester back in her life, yet with a few glasses of champagne she could throw caution to the winds, enjoy herself, give way. And I couldn't, damn it. You'd have to ladle a bottle of gin down my throat, and even then I'd probably just fall into a stupor. For the first time I felt angry at Stuart. Why didn't *he* do something? But the back rub had been good. Ketti obviously knew a few things.

BODY PARTS

I did go over to Gregory's finally. His father was walking out of the building as I got there and waved at me. Every time I saw him, I thought of Gregory's vituperative stories, of how he could only have sex with call girls; he looked normal to me.

Gregory's illness had left him even more gaunt and Charles Addamsish than ever. Not having seen him for a while, I'd forgotten his physical awkwardness, his huge hands that grasped me so fervently. He'd forgiven me my outburst on the phone and was only pleased to see me. While he'd been sick, he'd discovered Books on Tape and had listened to Kenneth Clark's autobiography and was now listening to something called *A Day in the Life of a Czar*. "It's wonderful," he said. "You can do it while you're in the bath, just resting, when your eyes are tired. . . . I went out for the first time and I listened as I went to the grocery store. Me with a Walkman! It's hard to imagine." Everyone seeing him probably assumed he was your average or not-so-average teenager listening to rock music.

We retreated into Gregory's room. The bed was made; it

136

was so neat it looked more as though he'd gone away than that he'd been sick for a couple of weeks. We sat down side by side. "I've missed you terribly," Gregory said intensely, his voice wavering the way it often did.

"I'm sorry I snapped at you on the phone," I said. "I really was concerned about Andria."

"Oh, of course, she's your friend. . . . It was all my fault. I try to be sensitive to your moods, but maybe it's never having had a girlfriend before. I still tend to be kind of self-absorbed."

I kissed him. "You're fine."

Gregory looked all around the room. "This may be the same thing, the same kind of horrible male insensitivity, but I just wondered . . . I mean, the parents are out, I'm not contagious anymore, and I feel great. Would you, do you think . . ."

"Sure," I said easily. "I'd love to." I thought of Stuart's remark that my liking Gregory was the most flattering thing that would ever happen to him, how I had transformed his self-image. Taking off my clothes, I felt, through his eyes, gracious, beautiful, effortlessly sexy. By now Gregory and I had figured out how to do it, as most people do. It wasn't always perfect, and there was always that thin sliver of knowledge that I wasn't in love with him, but it was good, it was satisfying.

Afterward, Gregory let out a great shuddering sigh. "God, I've thought about this nonstop for a week," he said.

"Even while you were listening to *A Day in the Life of a Czar*?" I teased.

"Even then. . . . It's good that I can keep my mind turning in the midst of all this erotic feeling. Otherwise I'd be a basket case."

"Your mind will always keep going," I assured him.

He frowned. "I know. . . . Sometimes I wish that weren't true, that I could just, you know, become an animal. Do you know what I mean?"

Did I ever! "I feel that too," I admitted.

"Of course, we're new at this," Gregory said. "We've

137

had all those years to develop our intellectual side, and only a few months for this. So maybe it takes time.''

I quoted Olive, who said we were sexual beings from the day we were born.

"You mean in some vague way, knowing we have bodies?'' Gregory said. "Oh sure. No, I meant—''

"I know what you meant.''

"The thing is, though,'' he said, "we're together because we have both . . . I mean, I like the fact that we can do this and then we can talk about poetry. I don't want just some . . . that other kind of woman, just—''

"I don't want that other kind of man either.'' I felt I was doing what I always did, not lying exactly, just giving him the wrong idea by being vague.

"The tragedy with my father,'' Gregory said, looking contemplatively at the ceiling, "isn't that he can't discuss poetry with a woman because he wouldn't know a poem from a pineapple, but that he just can't— He doesn't really see women as people.''

"How do you know all this?'' I asked.

"From my mother. . . . I guess she shouldn't tell me, but she has to tell someone, and I guess we have this natural sympathy. I mean, we both wish she hadn't married him, except I don't wish it quite as much because then I'd never have been born.''

"My father never tells me anything,'' I said. "I don't think he tells my mother much either.''

"Well, you have a normal family,'' he said.

"I don't!'' What did Gregory know about my family anyway? He'd met them only a few times. I felt my father was every bit as peculiar as Mr. Arrington, but in different ways. And it was true my mother wasn't a manic-depressive or anything that you could define clinically, but that didn't make her normal.

Gregory got up and went to get some poems he'd written while he was sick. For such a self-conscious person, he walked around in the nude gracefully. I couldn't help watching his balls swing back and forth. Maybe that's the way men can't help watching women's breasts. I tried to listen to the poems, but since some were obviously about me, it was a little hard to be objective. "I like the one about your body," I said.

"Well, I was thinking," he said. "What's so special about the parts of the body that always have to be covered up? What if we made a big fuss about showing an ear in public or an elbow? Then probably we'd get all excited just seeing someone's ear."

"But it's that they're connected to sex, isn't it?" I asked. "In a way ears and elbows aren't."

"Yeah, all I'm saying is that it's arbitrary. As objects, just if you, like, came upon them walking on a beach, I don't think you'd say, if you saw a penis, 'Wow,' and if you saw an ear, 'Who cares?' They're just differently shaped objects."

As Gregory had said, he'd had years to get excited about ideas like this.

A poem about finding body parts on the beach was the one Mr. O'Reilly liked, much more than he liked Gregory's more conventional sonnets about love. I went in to see him to go over my senior thesis, from which he'd weeded out what he called "the squishy ones."

"There *are* a few great erotic poems," he said. "Auden's 'Lullaby,' for one—'Lay your sleeping head, my love.' But that takes years and *years* of control and irony. Teenagers should be forbidden by law to go near the subject."

"That's so reductive," I said, "calling me a teenager. . . . I don't go around calling you a high school English teacher."

He smiled. "What do you go around calling me?"

"I don't call you anything. I take you as a separate individual, not as a member of a group."

"All I'm trying to do, Isabel, is to steer you away from years of writing about things just because you think you should, because you think 'one' should. . . . I wrote a great many novels in my twenties that some kind and wise person should have snatched from my typewriter and consigned to the ash heap, something I finally did myself years later."

I wondered what they had been about. "Maybe it was something you needed to get out of your system," I suggested.

"That's not what writing's all about," he said sternly.

"What was their . . . what were they about?" I felt tentative asking.

"All this kind of thing." He pointed to the poems of mine he'd weeded out. "Discovering one's sexual identity, the body, other people's bodies. If you'd read one, you'd be ashamed to be in the same room with me."

"I wouldn't at all," I said. "It would make you seem more human."

He raised an eyebrow. "Don't I seem human? I was laboring under the delusion that I did."

This was much like my conversations with my father, a funny kind of fencing match in which I advanced, we parried, he retreated. "You've helped me so much," I said impulsively. "I really appreciate it."

"Nonsense—you helped yourself. I was here to give you the occasional push in the right direction."

"I'll miss that," I said.

He shook his head. "You're not feeling nostalgic, are you? Don't. Nostalgia is a pernicious and false emotion. It's a blurring of reality."

I wanted, somehow, to turn this last meeting into something different from the others, something profound. "Do you think I made the right choice picking Swarthmore?"

"It's as good as any. You'll do fine there." He didn't say that he hoped I'd stay in touch, that he hoped I'd continue to show him future poems, that he looked forward to my having a brilliant career. It was as though the moment I left Whitman, I would cease to exist for him, or become one of those ghostly imaginary children he wrote about later.

SECRETS

Life resumed its more-or-less normal course. The "fearsome foursome" were whole again. One afternoon Ketti and I found ourselves together when Lois and Andria both had to leave early. It was so beautiful out, we decided to walk through the park. Ketti had been letting her hair grow and it was pulled back with a headband, showing her fine, lovely features. "If it weren't for what happened to Andria, this would have been such a perfect year," she said.

"But she's fine now," I said.

"Yes, but it's like a shadow." Then almost without a break she said, "Did you know Stuart's going to France? His father's sending him tickets."

Still that old coiling of my insides. "Yes, it sounds wonderful. Will you go too?"

"I have to work. . . . Anyway, I think now that we're graduating . . . well, we'll see. Who can tell? I'm very fond of Stuart, I really am. There's a lot more to him than meets the eye."

"But not in love?" I pursued, ashamed but unable to stop.

Ketti smiled. "Oh, sure, in love, but not . . . I mean when

141

I think of not seeing him over the summer, I'm not in despair. We don't have that bond, like Andria and Hal. . . . Well, isn't it pretty much like that with you and Gregory? Somehow I can't see you as a permanent couple.''

I was pleased. "Everyone else seems to think we're perfect together," I said ruefully.

"No," Ketti said, "I can't see that at all. I think you need someone more—expansive, exuberant. You've done a lot for Gregory, though. He always looked like such a weedy creature from outer space, and lately, he's kind of gotten his act together physically somehow.''

"It wasn't a charity case," I said. "I like him a lot. . . . And even the other part isn't bad." I felt self-conscious talking about physical things with Ketti.

"I can imagine. Guys like that who've stored it all up for so long can be great." She looked away. The flowering cherry trees were just beginning to turn. In a week the petals would glide to the ground. "I always thought it would be you and Stuart senior year," she said.

I looked fixedly at the trees. "Really?"

"Yeah, it just seemed— But I guess you never can predict." She gave me a glance that seemed probing.

"I think we're too much like brother and sister," I said. "It's a kind of closeness, but not that kind."

"Maybe for you," she said enigmatically.

"What do you mean?"

"I don't know. I just sometimes get the impression Stuart could see it differently if you'd let him."

"I don't think so. . . . He's had nine million opportunities." I thought of the night of the back rub.

"He's funny, though. I bet anything if I hadn't gone after him, like you suggested, nothing would have happened between us this year. He's the kind that needs encouragement.''

I laughed. "He'll get plenty of it in Marseilles with all those hot-eyed Mediterranean girls his father has lined up for him.''

"I didn't mean that kind of encouragement," she said, but let it drop.

That was what I always liked about Ketti, and I never knew

if it was sensitivity or if she didn't have the inclination to analyze things into the ground.

At home I found Gregory reading poetry to my mother. He'd taken to coming over when I wasn't there and reading to her while she ironed or folded the laundry.

My mother thought Gregory was wonderful. She'd forgotten that she'd once said how peculiar he looked. Now she only remarked that he was the most mature and thoughtful young man his age she'd ever met.

"I'm going to miss this so much," she said, "when you graduate."

Gregory was going to Columbia. "I can still come over and read," he said.

"Oh, but Isabel won't be here," she said. "And you'll be busy with other things, your studies."

"I'll come anyway. . . . You're the first person who's enjoyed listening to me read," he added with that ingenuousness so typical of him.

"I forced poor Sidney to listen to all of Jane Austen when we first married," she said, "and even some of E. M. Forster, but no one ever read to me."

"With poetry, reading aloud is crucial," Gregory said.

Gregory did with my mother what I never would have done—he actually read her first drafts of his poems and took her suggestions seriously. What was it about other people's mothers that made them seem so much better than your own?

GRADUATION

We graduated from Whitman, wearing our dark-purple robes and hats. I got the poetry prize, Andria was valedictorian and made the class speech. There was a prom, and even though we made fun of it, I went with Gregory and we both had a good time. He looked surprisingly handsome in a tuxedo. I had suspected he would either look good or impossible. Maybe in some way Stuart was right. Maybe my liking him had given Gregory some ineffable sense of self-confidence that actually showed. If so, it made my task of breaking up with him, which I felt I had to do that evening, all the more difficult. How terrible if, on hearing my decision, he crumpled up and became the old Gregory—even sobbed.

After the prom we went out with a bunch of the others to a club and danced some more. I danced with Stuart and murmured into his ear. "Tonight's the night I break up with Gregory."

"Poor guy." Stuart peered through the smoky room. "I guess he'll survive."

"You think?"

144

"Just do it gently, not your usual vicious one-two punch."

Gregory brought me home. Our apartment was extremely quiet; my parents had been in bed for hours. We sat on the couch and whispered. I was the one who felt tearful. "I'm going to miss you a lot," I began in a semi-whisper.

"Me too."

"But . . . well, we will be at different colleges and maybe, don't you think, we should—"

"Oh, of course," Gregory said. "I assumed that."

He was so composed I was a bit hurt. "Did you always assume it?"

"No, I just meant I don't want you to feel guilty. You've given me so much. . . . Well, maybe a girl can't understand what a difference that can make. I'll never forget you, Isabel."

"You've given me a lot too," I said, more to say something. I wasn't sure it was true or in the same way. "And anyway, we'll still be friends."

"Forever," he said, clasping my hands tightly.

So this is how a relationship ends, I thought. I was surprised it could be this painless. It was easier to end than it had been to begin. Would that always be true? I wondered. Suddenly I knew that I *had* gotten a lot from Gregory, even though my heart hadn't been wholly in this affair. I was glad I had had it.

We could have made love for old times' sake, but it was five in the morning and we were both pretty exhausted. We kissed at the door and I crept back to my room, feeling tired and keyed up at the same time. Twenty minutes later, as I was sinking uneasily into sleep, the door to my room opened. It was Stuart. He was still dressed in his tuxedo.

"It's six A.M.," I murmured.

He yawned. "I know . . . I feel rotten. I drank too much. I feel so sad, Iz. Comfort me."

"I'm exhausted; I just got into bed. Can't we talk in the morning?"

"It *is* the morning."

"In the afternoon?"

145

He was taking his tuxedo off. "Let me just stay here, please. We don't have to talk."

"Sure." Maybe it didn't seem that different from all our naps, or maybe I was so exhausted the whole scene was like something in a dream, where you can't remember later if it happened at all. It was only at ten in the morning, when I got up to go to the bathroom, that seeing Stuart, who was in his underwear, I remembered, and even then I was too sleepy to have any reaction except that he'd thrown his tuxedo on the floor and it was bound to get all wrinkled, whereas I, even in my exhausted state, had remembered to hang up my dress and put my earrings and necklace back in my jewelry box.

When we both woke up at one-thirty, the apartment was as silent as it had been the night before—evidently my parents had gone out. Oddly, we woke up at the exact same moment. We looked at each other warily.

"How do you feel?" I asked.

"Weird. . . . I think I better dunk my head in cold water."

"Just let me use the bathroom first." I peed and then brushed my teeth. Back in bed, I heard Stuart splashing around. He came back with his hair wet, toweled dry, drops flicking onto the pillow. I reached up and lightly touched his hair. "You're still wet," I said.

"Yes."

After fourteen years of hugs and glances and intense moments and fights and naps, it seemed odd that there could still be a moment that was different, the moment that all the others had been leading up to, but suddenly, undeniably, it was there. Stuart was so close to me, he reached out and touched my lips with his fingertip. "You brushed your teeth."

"So did you." I could smell the minty Crest smell.

And then we were both, almost for the first time in our lives, struck dumb. It wasn't just that there was nothing to say—I think we both knew if we said one word, we would fall back into some kind of verbal horseplay that would allow us to escape from what had to be done.

Instead we made love.

When it was over, Stuart smiled and said, "Did we survive?"

"I don't know."

And we laughed crazily, with relief.

"Was this what you had in mind when you came into my room last night?"

"No, I just wanted comfort. There wasn't a sexy thought in my head."

"And you want to be a shrink!"

"So sue me. . . . I thought you'd be asleep. I intended to sneak in, fall asleep next to you, that's all, that's it, your honor."

"Why did you brush your teeth?" I pursued.

"I hate that furry feeling they get in the morning, especially after I've been drinking. . . . Why did you brush yours?"

"Because I knew . . . and you did too, Stu. Why are you so piggishly stubborn?"

"If you hadn't said, 'You're still wet,' in that nice, tender, come-hither voice, nothing would have happened."

"I've said things like that to you a thousand times!"

"Come-hitherish things? Not that I've noticed."

I reminded him of the night of the back rub.

"That's a perfect example," he said. "Now if, after having the back rub, you had languorously rolled over onto your back and looked up at me with big, limpid eyes—"

"Why couldn't *you* have done something? Slipped your hand under my blouse, unhooked my bra?"

"I'm shy." He grinned.

"You're so full of shit. Really. You're just determined to play the innocent victim."

"Men are always the innocent victims. That's our lot in life. . . . Look at this year. First you sic Ketti on me when, if you hadn't, she never would have looked at me twice. Then you set out like a bulldog after poor old Gregory. . . . How did he take it, about your breaking up? Or haven't you told him yet?"

147

"He was fine. He said he knew it was inevitable."

Stuart sighed. "God, I feel so sorry for him. He's probably jumping off a bridge at this very moment."

"Nothing of the kind. He's grateful for what I gave him. . . . He was distressingly composed."

"What did you want? For him to fall sobbing at your feet?"

I smiled. "Yeah, kind of. . . . I was rotten to him, using him just to get even with you and Ketti."

"He loved every minute of it. And if you were jealous of Ketti, why did you suggest it in the first place? Why didn't you just tackle me yourself?"

"I was waiting for you to realize the inevitable. As far as *I'm* concerned, we've been engaged since first grade."

"You've only known that long?" Stuart looked surprised. "I decided at the end of that first year of nursery school. You were so good at obeying orders when we built things out of blocks, and you always brought such great oatmeal cookies to school. What more did I need in a wife?"

"But those were cookies my mother made," I objected.

"Yeah, but she can give you the recipe. And sure, I know you don't take orders as well as you did back then, but I can handle it. I need someone tough to keep me in line."

"Do you think we've moved too fast?" I asked, snuggling up to him.

"Fast! After fourteen years of foreplay? That'd probably get us into *The Guinness Book of Records*. The longest courtship in history."

I stared at the ceiling of my room, tracing all the shapes that had been there for as long as Stuart and I had known each other. Suddenly I flung myself across Stuart.

"What's this?" he asked, laughing.

I told him about my naptime fantasies. "What are we going to do now that fantasy has become reality?" I asked.

"We'll just have to move on to bigger and better," Stuart said.

I guessed that was what would happen, but right now I was completely satisfied with the moment. I knew something wonderful was starting, though in fact it had started ages ago.

About the Author

Norma Klein was born in New York City and graduated cum laude and a member of Phi Beta Kappa from Barnard College with a degree in Russian. She later received her master's degree in Slavic languages from Columbia University.

Ms. Klein began publishing short stories while attending Barnard and since then she had written novels for readers of all ages. The author got her ideas from everyday life and advised would-be writers to do the same—to write about their experiences or things they really care about.

Several of Norma Klein's books are available from Fawcett including MY LIFE AS A BODY, OLDER MEN, FAMILY SECRETS, and GIVE AND TAKE.

Ms. Klein died in 1989.